BASH and the Chicken Coop Caper

BASH and the Chicken Coop Caper

story by BURTON W. COLE
illustrations by TOM BANCROFT

B&H PUBLISHING GROUP
Nashville, Tennessee

Printed in the United States of America

978-1-4336-8070-0

Published by B&H Publishing Group
Nashville, Tennessee

Dewey Decimal Classification: JF
Subject Heading: CHRISTIAN LIFE—FICTION \ GOOD AND EVIL—FICTION \ PROVIDENCE AND GOVERNMENT OF GOD—FICTION

1 2 3 4 5 6 7 8 • 18 17 16 15 14

For Dad and Mom—Frank and Patti Cole—for the gallons of hot chocolate, games of Flinch, and the last nerves we four kids trampled while cooped up during the blizzards of 1977 and '78.

In memory of my son Joshua, called home at age nine before we were done playing. Daddy misses you, Champ.

Contents

Chapter 1

Snow Crazy

I perched atop the chicken coop and gulped puffs of frigid air. This was insane. I flapped mittened hands as I squawked at my crackpot cousin.

"Bash, we'll shoot off this roof at a thousand miles per hour, hurtle down the snowdrift mountain, smash through the maple tree, and blast our extreme sail-powered superboard supersleds to supersmithereens."

The Basher bobbed his ski-masked head. "Yeah. It'll be *awesome*."

"You think getting killed is awesome?"

Sebastian "Bash" Hinglehobb, my third cousin twice removed—but not removed far enough to prevent avalanches of disaster—swished his sled along a stretch of slick roof slope. "Chill, Beamer. If we crash and croak, we'll slide uphill all the way to heaven. Why worry?"

"Why? *Why?*" My head be-bopped so much that the wool scarf tucked under the edges of my glasses dropped from my face. Ice crinkles crackled inside my nose. "I'll tell you why. Because we might accidentally live. All our bones will be broken, but your mom will make us clean the barn anyway. I'll drag myself along the stinky, gooey, gross floor by my good elbow, pulling a wheelbarrow full of cow droppings with my teeth. I don't even want to think how I'll get the stuff into the wheelbarrow. *That's why.*"

Bash shaded his eyes against the miles of snow sparkling like millions of shaved-ice snow cones without the flavoring. Or the warmth. "You worry too much, Ray-Ray Sunbeam Beamer."

"Stop calling me that." I stomped my boot into the ice-sheened mattress of snow. "*Extreme, sail-powered superboard supersleds.* This has got to be your weirdest idea yet."

But the sooner we got it over with, the sooner I'd be inside with a mug of hot chocolate. I shivered. "Help me rig the sail."

"All right, Beamer. Prepare to have a blast." Bash chunked his sled into the two feet of snow on the roof and high-stepped his way toward me.

I rolled my eyes. Can eyeballs freeze solid? "Mashing all my bones in a sledding disaster sounds more like an explosion than a blast."

Bash strung pillowcase sails from masts built of rake handles and tomato stakes. I glanced over my shoulder at the other side of the chicken coop. I hated looking down. There was no snowdrift on that side, just a drop-off. A long, dizzy drop-off plunging far, far down into mounds of freezing, frigid . . . I squinted at the freezing, frigid mounds of snow. Were those . . . ?

I tapped Bash on his coat sleeve and pointed down. "Whose footprints are those?"

Bash scanned the trail through the drifts into the coop. "Ma's, probably. She collects the eggs early, before they freeze."

"No, *we* collect the eggs, during both morning and evening chores, remember? Aunt Tillie said that was our job. And those aren't our tracks. Basher, I think somebody ducked into your chicken coop."

Bash knotted baling twine onto the corners of the pillowcase sails. "Why? For eggs? We already got 'em." He tugged at the twine to make sure the string held. "Maybe Pops needed something in there. Who cares? C'mon, let's get this other sail on."

I peeked down again at the single set of tracks already drifting over and disappearing in the occasional sweeping gusts of wind. They didn't look like Uncle Rollie's footprints, but I'd never looked at his from on top the chicken coop roof before. I'd never been on top of the chicken coop before. Until the screaming blizzard dumped snow everywhere and blew it into a white ramp as tall as the eaves, we couldn't reach the roof. Not without a ladder. I hate ladders.

"You sure your mom won't care that we used pillowcases for sails?"

"She was too excited to get us out of the house. Didja notice how she set our coats and boots by the door?"

We'd been crammed inside a big ol' farmhouse for three days while snowstorms howled, pretty much ever since Mom and Dad dropped me off Friday. The weirder the adventure Bash thought up, the faster Aunt Tillie's eye ticked. By breakfast time today, her flapping eyelid threatened to cool off the fried eggs before she got them to the table. "Out, out, out. Go build a snowman or something. Anything."

Fine with me. We'd been stuck playing Candyland with Bash's three-year-old sister Darla, who made up her own rules. One more game of Candyland and I'd scream like, well, like the blizzard.

Now I wobbled atop the chicken coop roof. A wind gust whooshing with all the warmth of Popsicles packed in ice cubes blew my collar open and bit down my back. "Let's go play Candyland with Darla."

"Stop being a baby. This'll be awesome." Bash was shorter, skinnier, and younger than me—eleven. I'd turn twelve next month, three months before his birthday. Since I was older, I tried to keep him out of trouble with my smarter brains.

But January blizzards in northeast Ohio freeze brains, even smart ones like mine. I flung my fallen scarf back over my mouth and nose and tucked the top of the scarf under the bottoms of my glasses.

Chief Engineer Bash dug a hammer out of one deep snow coat pocket and nails and brackets out of the other. He mounted the rake handle masts to our two plastic sleds—his a blue toboggan style with curled-up front end, mine an orange saucer like an upside-down Frisbee. "I bet no one's ever rocketed off a chicken coop roof on a sail-powered superboard supersled."

I pulled off my mittens, shook my hands against the shock of refrigerator breath, and finished rigging my sail. "I bet no one else would be crazy enough." We were about to get extreme. Extremely stupid.

Then I spotted the polar bear.

Chapter 2

Sleds of Doom

"Are there polar bears roaming in your woods? Hungry ones?"

Bash shaded his eyes and stared off into the woods. "Aw, that's just the wind whipping up big gobs of snow. Besides, polar bears don't live in Ohio."

I took another long look. "I thought maybe one got lost." Wind gusts thumped the pillowcases. "Um, the sails are messed up. Maybe we better go inside."

Bash grabbed the dangling lines of baling twine and snapped open his pillowcase sail. "See, Beams? Use the twine to turn the sails and you just might be able to steer your supersled."

"Might?"

Chief Engineer Bash tugged his twine to the right. The sails billowed in the Arctic blasts. "Yep, they work like reins on a horse. Let's do it."

Nothing else came to mind except hiding under the bed, and to do that I'd have to get off the roof. And to get off the roof . . . I started to sit inside the saucer. Bash grabbed me by my padded coat shoulder with his gloved hand. "Nuh-uh. Remember the snowboard part? We gotta stand. It's in the rules."

"What rules? You made up the rules."

"It's on one of your video games, the snowboarding one. Snowboarders stand. Sitting's for wimps."

Oh, *now* he pays attention to a video game. "Um, I have to go inside now."

Bash pushed me.

"C'mon, ya sissy."

I tapped one boot inside the bright orange saucer. I dug the other foot into the snowy roof like an anchor. Another blast from the sky's giant air conditioner set on high tugged at my sled. Plastic saucers are slick. It almost took off. I shoved my anchor boot deeper into the snow bed and gaped down the steep drift. The whole farm seemed to be planted on a downhill. We'd fly for miles. *If* we didn't hit that teacher's-desk-hard maple tree.

Chief Engineer Bash huffed. "Well? Go, already."

I swung the sled at him. "It's your invention. You test it."

Bash flashed a look at the slope, then back at me. Snowflakes on his lashes nearly hid the frosty blue of his eyes. He blinked. "Company first. Besides, I gotta watch for flaws."

"*Flaws?* Um, maybe we should launch from that end of the chicken coop. No maple tree."

"Aw, the snowdrift's too flat down there. It doesn't even reach the roof. We'd hardly get any speed."

"I know." I shook my head, loosening the scarf again.

Bash pointed a gloved finger. "The snowdrift is a lot higher and steeper here. We probably won't stop until we're clear out in the hay field."

I stepped one boot into the saucer again. "I notice you keep saying *we*. So how come it's only *me* on a sled?"

Bash darted behind me and pushed. "Remember to steer around the maple tree!"

The orange saucer sled took off. "Hey, no fair! *Whoa!*"

I nearly tumbled off the sled. My anchor foot yanked out of the snow and landed on the sled. The slick saucer spun like a, well, flying saucer, with me as the alien. I hugged the rake handle mast and looked down. *A 720-degree spin right off the chicken coop roof.* I was going to be sick.

Bash cheered. "Wow, I gotta try that!"

Spinning in midair, I caught a glimpse of Bash pushing off on the long toboggan sled. Then I smacked down on the top of the ice-glazed snowdrift and shot down the wind-smoothed bank. I faced forward, but the pillowcase flapped in my eyes, blocking my aim. Another gust of wind roared against my back and the pillowcase billowed forward.

No, no, *no*. I rushed faster.

I peeked over the top of the mast. The maple tree came at me not at a thousand miles per hour like I'd told Bash—it was more like *two* thousand miles per hour, at least.

I grabbed a rigging line and leaned right. The saucer tilted into a sideways wheelie as a great blur of bark rushed by my left.

"Cool!" It sounded like Bash's voice. It could have been my guardian angel, who I'm sure jumped off the sled as soon as it spun down the chicken coop roof.

I wished I'd jumped off too.

I leaned left to flatten the saucer. I peeked over the top of the mast. A storage shed loomed. I tried to grab the knob on the door as I whizzed past but missed.

I barely skidded over an old corn picker partly buried by snow. I grabbed air three more times as I leaped two snow-drift ramps and a snow-covered tree stump. I was glad Aunt Tillie hadn't let us have any cookies, because I would be wearing them inside the woolen scarf.

Bash's Irish setter, Uncle Jake O'Rusty McGillicuddy Jr., gave chase to the edge of the hay field, then sat and watched me go.

The hay field. Bash was right. We *could* make it all the way to the hay field. Well, the edge of it, anyway. The field tilted. The sled dipped, cut the corner, and blasted straight for the frozen creek.

"Basher, you're a jerk!" I screamed through the scarf.

If I survived this, I'd smear his bed in maple syrup until he stuck, then spill his ant farm—ants, dirt, and all—all over him.

The supersled spun down the steep bank toward the iced-over creek that wound through Uncle Rollie's farm. *Yeow!* With a new gush of speed, I hit the ice and twirled like those fancy ice skaters on tip-toe. Only instead of wearing ice skates, I hugged a rake handle nailed to an orange plastic saucer on which I bucked in snow boots.

After what seemed like six or seven hours, the sled slowed from deadly doom ferocity to merely mind-numbing speed. I gulped down a breath of air.

Then another gust tore at the sail, and I burst down the icy track of the creek toward the big rock we sat on in the summer to catch frogs. I yanked on rigging rope, but it was too late. The sled slammed into the frog catching rock and stood on its rim.

I shot right down the barrel of the rake handle like I'd been fired out of a rifle. The pillowcases snagged on my arms and legs. One moment, I was Superman, flying through the air, pillowcase cape flapping in the wind. The next, I was an otter wearing dirty laundry, sliding on my belly right down the center of the frozen creek at roughly three thousand miles per hour.

The creek rounded a bend. I did not. *Ka-whumpf.* I whooshed up the creek bank and plowed headfirst into a snowdrift. There I stuck, buried nearly to my waist, my feet sticking straight out, twanging like an arrow shot into a target. I kicked so hard trying to get free that one boot flew off.

I wiggled there for what seemed like days. Talk about brain freeze. I had to look like a major dork. So this was how my life would end—as a snow bank snow stick with one boot on and one boot gone. I wouldn't even have a chance to staple all of Bash's shirts shut first. *Aargh.*

Something wrapped around my kicking legs.

The polar bear! I knew it. I had seen a lost polar bear, and he lived here now, and when he went to his snow bank refrigerator for a snack, there I was, sticking out the fridge door.

I kicked harder. The other boot flew away.

The bear roared. "Hey, cut it out."

Figures—the polar bear sounded like Bash. The last thing I'd hear before being eaten alive was my crazy cousin's annoying voice.

I burrowed further into the snowdrift. The bear tugged me back. Burrow. Tug. Burrow. *Big tug.* The bear popped me out of the snowdrift. I tumbled down the bank onto the bear.

"Get offa me."

Talking polar bears?

I opened my eyes.

Bash. With a grin so big I could read it through his ski mask. "That was *super awesome,* Beamer!"

I flung snow at him. "Where are my boots?"

"Here. Supersledding without boots—not many kids have the guts to do that."

"Go poke your eye out with an icicle. How come you didn't catch me?"

Bash ducked his head. "Aw, I fell off my extreme sail-powered superboard supersled on the first drift. I didn't get to have any of the fun you did."

I hardly felt the boots as I wrestled them onto numb feet. "I could cram you into the snow bank and pull off your boots. Go ahead. It'll be fun."

"Nope. I wanna do it the way you did."

We trudged back to the house, dragging shards of sled, chunks of rake handle and pieces of pillowcases behind us. Bash kicked at a bush and watched the explosion of snow. "You gotta teach me how to snowboard like that. You act as boring as rutabagas, but you're a daring dude, cuz."

I poked my glasses up on my nose and glared. "Climb up onto the barn and it'll be my turn to push you off. You won't even need the sled."

Aunt Tillie poked her head out the back door as we

plowed our way through the yard. "Boys, hot chocol . . . *Are those my good pillowcases?*" Her eyelid flickered, then took off into a full-flighted flapping.

I whispered through my scarf. "I don't think pillowcases were part of 'anything to get us out of the house.'"

Bash wilted a bit. "I wish adults said what they meant. It's like they're trying to trap us."

I had a few traps I wanted to lay for Bash myself. But they'd have to wait—probably for about sixty-three years, which is about how long I figured Aunt Tillie would ground us.

It didn't seem the right time to ask her about the odd footprints tracking to the chicken coop. Maybe later, when my toes warmed up and Aunt Tillie cooled down. Which might take till the first robin of spring.

Whose footprints were they? Why was someone sneaking around the chicken coop?

Chapter 3

Fruits and Knuckleheads

Minutes after being chased up to Bash's room, I slipped the tips of my fingers from beneath layers of quilt, snagged the edge of the comforter, and rolled until I smacked against the wall. I wasn't sure I'd ever be warm again, but I meant to try.

Bash snickered. "You look like a caterpillar in glasses, Ray-Ray Sunbeam Beamer."

I didn't bother to tell him again to stop calling me that. I could use a nice, hot sunbeam right about now. I tried to think about something other than icicles. Like the footprints. Something, or somebody, went into the chicken coop and didn't come out. I shivered. From the cold, I mean. "What about those huge footprints leading up to the chicken coop?"

Bash shucked the sweatshirt Grandma gave him for Christmas a couple weeks ago and dropped it and himself to the floor. "What about them?"

"Shouldn't we tell your parents?"

"Why?"

"Maybe an omelet bandit's trying to steal your mom's laying hens. Maybe a feather monster in boots who eats chickens in one gulp broke in—and is looking for some kids to nibble for dessert."

"Don't be silly. Monsters don't eat chickens." The Basher scooped up a basketball, flopped onto his back, and tossed the ball as close to the ceiling as he could without actually chipping the paint. We'd worked on ceiling tosses when we got grounded last summer. We were experts.

I squinted at Bash. "How do you know *this* monster doesn't eat chickens?"

"Chickens are noisy. We woulda heard them."

"Not if they got eaten."

"Then you'd hear the monster burp. Don't sweat it."

Sweating definitely was something I wasn't doing, not even wrapped in the color-splashed sweatshirt Grandma gave me for Christmas. But I worried about the chickens.

Bash rolled over and pulled his Bible with the cartoon drawings on the cover from beneath his bed. He always slid it under there when he finished reading so it would be easy to reach. I was afraid to look under the other bed, the one I used when I stayed over. Who knew what Bash had stashed beneath me.

Bash scooped the Bible into his lap. "We'll check the chickens in a couple hours when we do evening chores. Besides, we have plans."

"Yeah, build an igloo. In Florida."

"Not that one. Harvesting fruits. You're a farmer now, remember? You let Jesus into your heart when you stayed here last summer. The Farmin' and Fishin' Book—"

I sighed. "It's called the Bible."

Evangelist Bash jumped up and paced the floor. "I keep tellin' you, the Bible is full of stories about farmin' and fishin'. That's why we farm boys understand it so well."

He blew messy strands of his flyaway straw-colored hair out of his eyes. "David the sheep farmer knocked down the giant Goliath with a slingshot. Moses the sheep farmer made bunches and bunches of frogs take over a whole nation."

"Shepherd. Sheep farmers are called shepherds. And God sent the frogs, not Moses."

"Moses got to tell the king to watch where he stepped or he'd squish frogs 'tween his toes."

Bash flopped to the floor and slapped his Bible open across his lap. "Anyway, the Farmin' and Fishin' Book says when we belong to God, we plant seeds, grow fruit, and fish for people."

I froze a shake in mid-shiver. "We jumped off the roof of the chicken coop on sail-powered supersleds. What kind of seed, fruit, or fish do you call that?"

His blue eyes sparkled—they always did around trouble. "We whooped and laughed the whole time, Beamer. That's the fruit of joy."

If I pulled down the curtains, could I wrap up in them too? "I don't remember the laughing part. But I think I whooped."

"You screamed."

"Did not."

"Yep, you did."

Bash stopped flipping pages. He jammed a finger in his Bible. "Look, right here in Galatians 5:22 and 23, it says harvest the fruit of the Spirit. That's farm talk."

"From a kid with banana mush for brains."

He traced the lines across the page. *"But the fruit of the Spirit is love, joy, peace, patience, kindness, goodness, faith, gentleness, self-control."*

I rolled out of one layer of comforter. "You do joy. I'm busy working on self-control."

Bash chewed on his tongue for a moment. "Maybe you don't have joy crossed off the list. You screamed too much."

"I didn't scream. I whooped. Besides, my feet froze. My boots fell off."

"You kicked them off when you were playing human dart boy in the snow bank."

I unrolled another layer or two, snagged a pillow, and hurled it at Bash. He flung both mine and his at me. Just the pillows. No cases. Aunt Tillie said since we turned our pillowcases into sails, we'd just go without.

Bash set down his Bible. "It'll take days for the plows to clear away all the snow from the blizzard, maybe a whole week. You're stuck here. So we've got lots of time to become great Spirit fruit farmers. Ray-Ray Sunbeam Beamer, we're gonna pick every one of those fruits before the side roads are opened—even if it hurts."

"With you, it usually does. And stop calling me that. My name's Raymond. Keep it up and I'll call you by your real name, Mr. Sebastian Nicholas Hinglehobb."

The Basher rolled over in a burst of laughter—the cackling of a miniature madman. "Raymond William Boxby, when you call somebody names, you can't use their real one. That's silly."

I snatched both pillows and got ready to fire them back. I wished I had some rocks to put in them. But then I felt a stab in my heart. A good Christian probably doesn't want to knock his cousin's block off. This saved stuff's hard. I lowered the pillows and sighed.

Evangelist Bash pumped his fist. "You just did self-control. Check it off the list." Then he rolled his dirty socks into a ball and beaned me right between the eyes.

"Uncheck it!" I dove to put him in a sleeper hold. I wasn't going to harvest patience or gentleness either.

Aunt Tillie hollered up the stairs, "Boys! Knock it off. Time for chores."

Great. I just finished melting the glacier off my body and now I had to clomp through the snow again to help Bash in the barn. And follow the strange footprints into the chicken coop. Big footprints. Maybe monster-sized.

The shivering kicked in again.

Chapter 4

Mystery in the Chicken Coop

It was only six o'clock, but the Monday afternoon sun had already sunk behind distant snowdrifts. I sucked in a painful lungful of knife-sharp cold air. "Maybe we should wait till morning to feed the chickens again."

"Baby."

Me? I wasn't the one chewing his tongue like a pacifier. Bash chomped away, his cheek bulging beneath the ski mask. He chugged a shovel through waist-deep snow—he left most of the big drifts alone—toward the chicken coop. I shuffled behind.

"Your dad already plowed a straight path with one of the tractors."

"This way we get to watch the snow fly," Bash said, barreling forward. He whirled, heaving a shovelful of snow at me. "Grab a shovel and dig your own trails."

I brushed away the Bash flurry. "Weirdo."

The mysterious footprints had vanished, swirled away in the afternoon snowing and blowing. Uncle Rollie probably never saw them when he plowed.

We swooped inside the chicken coop and switched on the light. Enough nesting boxes for a hundred or more chickens lined one long wall. Three dozen chickens clustered together in feathery balls on rods and ladder roosts, their heads nearly pulled inside their bodies like downy turtles. Chickens don't mind snow so much, but unlike us, they're smart enough to not go outside in a blizzard.

Bash leaned his shovel against the wall and tugged off his ski mask. "You get the broom this time. I'll stuff more straw in the boxes."

"I swept last night. It's your turn."

Bash jammed a knee into the side of a bale of straw and yanked back on the string holding the bale together. The bale bent, then straw exploded all over as Bash burst open the bundle. "Too late. I've already started. You sweep."

"Cheater."

Chickens are messy. The feathers all over the floor smell dusty and can send a kid with allergies into sneezing fits. The other stuff chickens drop smells almost as bad as rotten eggs. Fortunately, cold freezes the smell pretty well.

I swished the broom. Bash's favorite bird-brain, Mrs. Finley Q. Ruffeather Beakbokbok, flapped from the roost, strutted across the floor at me and pecked at my toes. She was called an Easter-egger hen because she laid big green eggs. The other hens laid brown, tan, pink, or white ones. Except for Polly Pufflecheeks Piffles, the other Easter-egger hen. She laid blue eggs.

I felt Mrs. Beakbokbok's sharp beak right through Uncle Rollie's barn boots that I borrowed for chores. "Cut it out." I shooed away the chocolate-colored chicken with the chipmunk cheeks.

I swept past the roosts stuffed with chickens. "How come you feather dusters can't clean up after yourselves?"

A whumping like that of a small helicopter or a giant bat whooshed above me. A gush of air washed down on my face. Something heavy plopped onto my head. Claws—four of them on each foot—dug through my wool hat. A chicken had chosen my head as her egg.

"Hey, get off me!" I dropped the broom and swatted above my head until I came down with a double handful of huge red hen. She tilted her head and regarded me with gold-rimmed eyes. Then her beak shot forward and pecked the center of my glasses.

"Yipe!" The hen wriggled through my gloves, flapped to the floor, and ran off with my glasses dangling from her beak.

My blueberry-brained cousin laughed so hard he could barely scoop up the hen and retrieve my glasses. "Ol' Queen Clucken Henny Penny of the Red Rhodes fooled you, Beamer. Here're your peepers."

I grabbed my glasses from Bash's gloved hand and jammed them onto my face. "Chicken toes hurt." I rubbed my head.

Bash set down the hen. "Hey Beamer, what do you call a crazy chicken?"

I circled around the hen. "Queen Clucken Henny Penny of the something or other."

"No, a cuckoo cluck." Bash crowed and slapped his thigh.

"That's just dopey." I swept and scraped chilled glop and goop all the way to the chicken-wire-enclosed pen against the far wall where Aunt Tillie stored bags of feed, more straw bales, and other supplies for her hens.

Bash stuffed fresh straw in the boxes. "How long do chickens work?"

I stopped in mid-feathery sweep. "Um, Bash."

"Around the cluck. Ha!"

"Bash?"

"Around the cluck. Get it, Beams?"

I ignored the fowl joke. "Are you wearing your gloves?"

"Yep."

"Both of them?"

"Well, duh. Why?"

"Somebody's been sleeping in the chickens' bed." I pointed the broom at the pen. "And there's his glove."

Bash unlatched the pen door and snatched up the dark blue, fuzzy glove. "I don't see Goldilocks."

"Look at the indents in the straw. Somebody was lying there."

Bash lugged one of the half-dozen heavy feed sacks off the floor and thumped it down a few inches away onto one of the depressions in the straw. "Or, Sherlock, the bumps in the night were made by chicken food. One here . . ." He picked up the bag and thunked it down again. One here, and . . ." He moved the sack again. "A third one here."

I studied the pen. "I don't remember seeing those bumps yesterday when we fed the chickens."

"Didja look?"

"Well, no, not really."

Bash nodded and grunted the feed bag back into place. "You read too many mysteries, Beamer."

"What about the glove? Chickens don't wear gloves do they?"

"Not unless they're cold." Bash picked up the glove, flipped it from one side to the other, and dropped it again. "Nope, our chickens prefer yellow gloves."

"Knock it off, knucklehead. You know what I mean. Whose glove is it?"

Bash left the pen and latched the door behind him. "Who cares? Ma or Pops probably dropped it months ago. C'mon, finish the sweeping. We still gotta help Pops with the milking."

"Meaning you're going to make me get the pitchfork and shovel and clean up behind the cows again."

Bash grinned. "I love it when you visit the farm. It's so much fun."

I sneezed as I swatted chicken dust with the broom. "Yeah. Loads."

We bundled up for the trip to the cow barn. I took one more look at the glove lying in the straw. It hadn't been there this morning. I would have noticed. Wouldn't I? First footprints. Now a glove. Weird.

I turned to ask Bash, but he was gone. I slapped the light switch. "Take your glove and go home," I yelled into the darkness of the chicken coop.

Something pecked at my foot. Probably Mrs. Beakbokbok. I decided not to stay around to find out.

Chapter 5

Camels and Damsels in Distress

"Beamer! Guess what we're going to do today."

I swatted at the hummingbird-on-a-sugar-high voice that hovered above me the next morning. Shouldn't humming birds have buzzed south for the winter by now? Maybe I could mail this one. If I could stamp him.

The buzzing dove in for another raid on my sleep. "Ray-Ray Sunbeam Beamer, get up, get up, *get up*! We get to do the best thing ever today."

I rolled over, peered through the crack of one crusted

eyelid and said the only thing that made sense at that hour: "Mmrggwhp?"

Bash grabbed my shoulder and shook it like he was trying to yank a monster icicle off the eaves. "Don't you want to know what we're going to do today right after chores?"

"Wind you up in a woolen scarf and swing you over the pigpen so they can play tetherball?"

"Nope. But we oughta try that with you sometime."

"Go 'way." I rolled back toward the wall and mashed my face into my pillow—which did not have a pillowcase.

"But you haven't heard what we're going to do today."

"Sleep. Stay warm. Eat cookies."

"We're gonna be like knights and rescue damsels in distress."

I groaned. "Do you even know what a damsel is?"

"Sorta like a camel, I think. Anyway, it's the only thing knights rescue, so that's what we got to do."

If it's possible to roll your eyes while they're squeezed shut, I did. "The roads are closed. No camels can get through. Plus, there aren't any camels in Ohio. Go back to bed, Basher."

Rescue Ranger Bash shook my shoulder again, yanking me back around. "C'mon, Beamer, you know whenever you stay overnight with me that we have to get up in the morning to feed the cows, muck the pig pen, and gather eggs in the chicken coop."

The chicken coop. I sat up, spilling blankets into my lap.

"Bash, did you remember to tell your folks about the glove and the footprints?"

"Beamer, there's four feet of snow on the ground. Everybody and everything leave footprints everywhere."

"Yeah, but—"

"An' it's a farm. You can find old gloves, old rags, an' old socks in pretty much every building on the place."

I shoved my glasses in place, even though it meant seeing Bash in focus. "Old socks?"

"Grass feels great on bare feet in the summer. But sometimes I forget where I left my socks."

"Um, with your shoes?"

"Yeah, right. Anyway, let's go. Those camels won't rescue themselves."

I swatted his hand off my sleeve. "If the camels in distress were dumb enough to leave the desert for this, they don't need a rescuer, they need a guidance counselor. And a GPS."

"Camels don't have GPS. That's why we gotta do it. And we get fruit."

I flopped back onto my pillow and clamped my hands onto my head. "Hold on a sec. Damsels in distress riding camels in distress without GPS wandered out of the desert, got stuck in the snow, and now they're waiting to be rescued at a fruit stand? In the middle of a blizzard?"

Bash tilted his head and stared at me with the same blank look as Henny Penny Whatever the Chicken. "You're weird, Ray-Ray Sunbeam Beamer."

"Stop calling me that!"

Bash cackled. "Fruit of the Spirit, of course. We picked the joy fruit with the supersleds. You picked self-control yesterday, then lost it. When we rescue the damsels on camels, we'll harvest goodness for our fruit basket. C'mon."

The fruit basket scampered from the room. Footfalls clattered down the stairs. The yummy scents of sizzling sausage, warm biscuits, and frying eggs wafted up the stairs, curled around my nose, and tickled my tummy. I sighed, shoved aside the pile of blankets and shuddered as my feet touched the floor. I needed my Christmas sweatshirt from Grandma today. It was big, fluffy, splashed in reds and greens and blues and yellows and purples and oranges, and—most importantly—it was warm.

Footfalls charged back up the stairs. Bash poked his applesauce head through the doorway. "Remember to stash extra biscuits in your pockets. The camels and damsels will be hungry." And he was gone. I twisted both fingers in my ears, trying to stop the echoes of Bash's buzzing. Rescuing damsels. Why couldn't the camels just eat the fruit? I looked up and breathed a prayer to my Best Friend: "Dear Jesus, please don't let me get killed today."

We burst into the chicken coop and stomped the snow off our boots. Roosting chickens squawked, and a couple puffed up and shook off a shower of feather puffs. I shivered and glared at Bash. "How come you can't shovel in a straight line? It's cold out there."

Bash tossed the snow shovel to the floor. "Ya gotta admit it was a pretty cool figure eight."

"Not cool. Cold."

"Beamer, it's warmer today. 'Sposed to climb all the way to the mid-thirties."

"So's your refrigerator."

Bash bounded to the storage pen. "Told ya. No sleeping beauties, and the gloves are still here."

"Gloves?" I tiptoed to the pen. Two blue gloves lay folded on the back of a burlap feed sack. "Bash, there are *two* gloves."

"Well, duh. One glove won't do much good."

"But last night there was only one glove. On the floor."

Bash scratched his ear. "Are you sure? I thought there were two. Didn't you say two?"

"No, I did not." I backed away from the pen, bent my knees in the ready-to-run position and scanned the chicken coop. No more gloves. No monsters. Nothing else odd. Even the bumps in the straw in the pen looked the same.

Bash followed my darting gaze. "See, Beams. Everything's just like last night."

I stomped to the broom and shovel and swept so hard that chickens scattered from the dust cloud. I didn't use the shovel. There weren't many chicken droppings to scrape up this morning.

Bash counted nineteen eggs—tans, browns, whites, pinks, speckled, and one green and one blue—into the collection basket. I stopped sweeping, took the basket from Bash and recounted. Nineteen. "Shouldn't there be twenty-four?"

"Usually. The other twelve hens lay their eggs in the afternoon. Thirty-six hens, thirty-six eggs a day." Bash tucked a thick towel over the basket like a blanket. "Sometimes a hen misses a day. It is pretty cold."

"Yeah, but—"

"Bwak, bwak-bwak bwaaaak!" Mrs. Beakbokbok tore after me, her flapping wings kicking up clouds of straw, feathers, and chicken dust. I ran. "Call her off, Bash! I'm going to drop the eggs."

Bash cuddled a black-and-white speckled hen he called Cheryl Checkers P. Featherchecker. They both clucked and cackled as I sped past.

"Hey Beamer, why do chickens lay eggs? 'Cause the eggs would break if they dropped them. Don't drop the eggs, you big chicken."

"Not funny," I yelled on my second lap around.

Bash dropped to his knees and cooed at the brown bird. "C'mere, Mrs. Finley Q. Ruffeather Beakbokbok." She stopped chasing me, strutted over to Bash, and scratched her head against his cupped glove. The crazy cuckoo cluck couldn't decide if she was an attack dog that cackled or a cuddly kitten that laid eggs.

Bash scratched Mrs. Beakbokbok's head behind her little red comb. "Nice chicken. If you stop picking on the city kid, I'll find you some bugs to eat. How 'bout that?"

"You're a couple of turkeys," I growled.

A few scatterings of feed and straw later, we bundled out of the chicken coop. I fell in behind Bash and his zigzag shovel as they burrowed a new route to the cow barn. While he shoveled, I thought. The more I thought, the more I knew I wasn't wrong. "No gloves were there Saturday or Sunday. And only one was there yesterday. I know it." I kicked a snow clump at Bash to make sure he was listening. Bash and shovel plow spun around. "Give it up, Beams. You're not as smart as you think you are."

I leaped over the blade. A rain of snow from the shovel tumbled down my boots. Yuck. "I'm smarter than you. Besides, if you didn't believe me, why'd you look?"

"To prove you're a peach pit."

I crossed my arms. "I'm not crazy."

"That's not what I heard."

"You think this is funny."

"Everything's fun when you let it be, Beamer. C'mon, let's finish chores so we can get to the rescuing."

I waved my arms. "With what, Sir Bash the Bobblehead? You don't have a horse."

Bash turned and dug the snow shovel into another drift. "We don't need a horse. We've got a pig."

Chapter 6

The Pig-Powered Ambulance Sled

We stomped into the cow barn, where I hung the egg basket on a nail before facing the brainless wonder. "A pig-powered what?"

"Ambulance sled. How else did you think we could rescue damsels in distress?"

Bash opened bunches of hay bales, and we heaved clumps of the stuff along the front end of the stalls as breakfast for the cows. I scratched one of the cows on her black-and-white forehead. "I thought we were rescuing camels without GPS. And what's a pig-powered ambulance sled?"

"You'll see. It'll be awesome. C'mon. Keep up."

The front end done, we used pitchforks and shovels to clean out the backside of the stalls. I kept the scarf wrapped over my nose. The stink from the backside of sixty cows isn't the kind of thing a guy likes to inhale when huffing and puffing from hard work.

An hour later, I dropped into a pillow of straw inside a little pen where a six-month-old calf named Amy romped. I was kind of like her uncle since she was born when I stayed on the farm last summer.

"Hiya, girl. What's new?"

The reddish-haired calf bounded over my outstretched legs a couple times before chomping my wool hat off my head. She skittered to the other side of the pen. I dove after her. "Hey, give me that."

Bash leaned over the pen. "Stop fooling around with the tug-o-war. Take that basket of eggs to Ma and grab a spare blanket from my closet. I'll grab the other supplies from the garage. Meet me at the pig pasture. We've got victims to find and rescue."

I wrestled my hat out of Amy's mouth and pulled it down over my ears. Yuck. Calf slobber.

Fifteen minutes later—first I had a quick mug of hot chocolate with big, fat marshmallows—I found Bash outside the pig hutches looping baling twine behind the front legs of his three-hundred-pound, rust-colored riding hog. "This will be awesome. Gulliver J. McFrederick the Third will pull our sled down the road, and we can look for victims to rescue."

I rubbed the shaggy back of the hog. "Why not just call him Gully?"

Bash continued looping the twine, this time in front of Gulliver's stubby pig legs, fashioning a harness. "What fun is a short name when we can make up long, fancy ones?"

I smacked my forehead a couple times with a mittened hand. It didn't help. Bash's logic still made no sense. I handed him the blanket, the one with pictures of cowboys riding bucking broncos. "The blizzard was two days ago. Why didn't we rescue anyone then?"

Bash refolded the blanket and smoothed it across Gulliver's back and sides. A couple more loops of baling twine kept the blanket in place. "You can't rescue victims during a storm. You have to go after."

"So why didn't we go yesterday?"

"Didn't think of it then."

"You've got all the smarts of a bushel of apples. Wormy ones."

Gulliver snuffled his snout into a snow clump, grunted, raised his thick head and shook it. Snow flew from his nose and his floppy ears clapped against his face. He grunted at me, his mouth crinkled into a grin, like always.

Rescue Ranger Bash fastened the far ends of the twine to the runners of a long, wooden sled. "When we find victims, they'll probably have broken legs. And be buried in avalanches. We'll pull 'em out, load 'em onto the sled like it's a big stretcher and pull 'em to safety."

"What if they don't want to be rescued by a pig? Or his hog?"

"Ha. If I'm a pig, you're a chipmunk. Anyway, the victims won't know if we're pigs or 'munks. They'll be unconscious."

"How do you know?"

Rescue Ranger Bash duct-taped a glove box emergency kit to the front of the sled. "If they were awake, they would walk to safety on their own."

"Or pass out when they see a pig coming. And his hog."

Bash heaved the roll of duct tape at me. It bounced off my padded parka. He pointed at the sled. "Shut up and get on the ambulance."

"What ambulance?"

"That one. Where the medical kit is. You're riding. I'm driving."

I eyed the sled tied to the hog. Rescue Ranger Bash flicked his gloves at me, motioning me to sit down. "You know why we're doing this, don't you, Beamer?"

I tapped the sled with my boot. "Because we're idiots?"

"Because rescuing unconscious people with broken legs from avalanches is good. We're going to harvest the fruit of goodness."

I rolled my eyes. "You're a Grape-Nut."

Bash slung his leg over Gulliver's back. The trained riding pig in a blanket perked up. His natural grin seemed to grow bigger. The hog's, I mean. I couldn't see Bash's face through the ski mask, but I'd seen him ride Gulliver lots of times, and I knew his goofy grin. Bash's, I mean.

Maybe someday Uncle Rollie and Aunt Tillie would get Bash a pony.

Bash took hold of Gulliver's floppy ears, tapped his blanketed sides with his boots and yelled, *"Giddyup."* Gulliver shot through the open pasture gate, a rusty pork barrel churning through the snow, sometimes hopping, sometimes tunneling, but always smashing a trail through drifts and driveway toward the road.

He ran even faster after I tumbled off the bucking ambulance sled into a snow bank. *"Yeow."*

I dug myself out and chased after them. Gulliver squealed. Bash squealed. I huffed. Gulliver grunted. Bash grunted. I puffed. "Wait up!"

I launched myself at the sled and landed belly flop first. All I could see in front of me were galloping pig feet, a swishing curly-cue tail, and, well, a wiggling rump roast.

Suddenly we were a pig-powered ambulance sled squealing down the road. I was the one squealing.

Bash's voice floated above me. "Keep an eye out for victims."

All I saw were hooves and hind end. If you're not the lead hog, the view doesn't change.

"Where are wee-wee-wee?" The sled banged over snow bumps, making my question come out like the little piggy on his way home. Only we were going the wrong way.

"This way leads to Jig and Jag's farm."

I'd never seen so much snow all at once. On either side of me loomed towering walls of white, thrown up by the plows that had cut through the drift-buried road that morning. I bounced right, then swished left over the snow-chunked road. "My stomach hur-hur-hurts."

We trotted past where a side road was supposed to be. Clogged. The plows weren't working those yet.

A hand clomped me atop my wool hat. "C'mon, Beamer, sit up and search for victims to rescue."

"Slo-oh-oh-ow dow-own."

Gulliver slowed to a mosey. Carefully, I tucked my legs under me and knelt on the sled. I let go with one mitten. I loosened my grip on the other side and caught my first view of life overtop the pig. Twisted in his blanket saddle, my freakazoid cousin stared down at me, blue eyes glittering through the eye holes of his ski mask.

Over his shoulder, a yellow car skidded toward us. I waved my free hand frantically. "Bash. Car. Steer the sled!"

A horn blared. *"Blaaaaat."*

Bash yelped. *"Hang on."*

Gulliver squealed. *"Rweeeeet."*

The car slid into a spin.

Rescue Ranger Bash had found his victim.

Chapter 7

This Little Piggy Played Ambulance

Gulliver leaped to the left. The sled bucked to the right and flew into the air. I somersaulted over it.

Whump. The car plunged into a wall of plowed snow.

Clump. The sled crashed onto the ice-glazed road.

Woomp. Bash on the hog jumped into a snow wall.

Fwump. I flew several inches into the snow bank on the other side of the road and stuck.

Silence. Then the Basher—still atop Gulliver's blanketed back—popped from the pig-and-boy-shaped indentation in the snow like a plastic toy from a mold. *"Awe! Some! Ride! Dude!"*

I dropped from the snow wall. "What kind of chipmunk brain are you? You almost got us killed." I gasped. "The car."

Bash tumbled off Gulliver and scrambled toward the car. "Fruit of goodness, here we come. I told you we'd find victims to rescue."

I shook the sled free and stumbled after him. "You said *find* victims, not *make* them."

A sunshine yellow car, buried from snout to windshield, poked out of the snow wall, backside an inch off the road, wheels still spinning.

Bash yanked open the driver's side door. I took the passenger side. A dark-haired lady in a red jacket slumped over the steering wheel, sobbing. A tanned girl bundled in sweaters patted the lady's back and glared at me with grizzly bear brown eyes. She swatted my nose. "I'd just gotten Mom to stop crying, and then you guys and that pig . . ." She scowled and thwacked my nose again.

I covered my nose. "Cut it out. *He* drove the pig."

Rescue Ranger Bash knelt to touch the woman's shoulder. "Where's it hurt, lady?"

Her whole body shook. Grizzly Girl wrapped herself over the woman's side and shivered. "It's okay, Mom. We'll be okay. Want me to swat the Pig Boy for you?"

The woman shook her head on the steering wheel.

The girl glowered at Bash. "You wouldn't be attacking us with a pig if my daddy was here."

I scanned the car. "Where's your dad?"

She whirled at me. I jumped out of nose-thwacking reach. "Daddy died six months ago. He got real sick." Her eyes dropped for a second, before boring into me in brown fire.

"I try to take care of Mom. I hold her hand, and I hug her. We were doing okay today—before you and Pig Boy made her cry again."

"I, uh . . ." I reached into my pocket for rescue provisions. "Biscuit?"

A sob that sounded like it started from way down in the driver lady's tennis shoes rolled up her back, shook her shoulders, and shuddered back down to the floorboards until it filled the car. It jammed a lump in my throat.

The girl stopped glaring and hugged her mom. I stuffed the biscuit back into my pocket. Bash scrunched down to look up into the lady's face. "Maybe you have a broken leg. I've never set a broken leg before. I probably can with some boards and duct tape. Ray-Ray, hand me the duct tape."

"I don't have any."

"I gave it to you."

"You *threw* it at me. It was your duct tape. I left it in the snow."

Bash patted the woman's arm. "Don't worry, lady, I can tie it with baling twine instead."

The woman peeked at Bash. "It's . . . I'm . . . It's okay. My legs are fine. It's just that . . . What are we going to do? We lost our home. We moved into an old trailer up here last week."

Rescue Ranger Bash nodded like a doctor listening to a list of aches and pains. "I heard somebody moved into the old Rodriguez place back in the woods. He used it for a hunting camp when he came up from Florida."

The lady sniffled. "My husband's uncle. We didn't have anywhere else to go. Then the blizzard." She shivered. "We don't have winter coats. We don't have heat. I can't get to town for food. All that snow. My kids are so cold."

Kids? I creaked opened the back door. A little boy with socks on his hands blinked from a car booster seat. I waved. "Um, hi, kid." I dug into my pocket. "Biscuit?"

Now what? I stepped around the open door to ask the girl. That's when Gulliver, sled clumping along behind him, crawled into the backseat and plopped his massive, shaggy red head across the boy's lap. Gulliver sighed. The little kid giggled and flipped Gulliver's floppy ears. The kid fed Gully the biscuit.

Grizzly Girl tugged at the lady's jacket. "Mom, there's a giant pig in our car. I think he wants to eat Tyler."

The woman spun around and gasped. Gulliver sighed at her with his piggy grin as the boy giggled and scratched the hog's head. A slow smile reached up to greet a tear rolling down the woman's cheek. "A Duroc hog. I used to raise them when I was a little girl. They are the sweetest pigs ever."

She unclipped her seat belt and scooted around in her seat to rub Gulliver's slobbery snout with her bare fingers. "And the smartest too. See, Lauren, how he's keeping Tyler warm?"

The lady traced a finger over Gulliver's grinning face. "What's his name?"

"Raymond. But we call him Ray-Ray Sunbeam Beamer for short."

"Not me, doofus. She means Gulliver." I couldn't reach Bash to slug him, so I helped the lady chuck Gulliver under the chin instead. "The pig's name is Gulliver. I'm Ray. The nitwit is Bash. He calls the pig Gulliver J. McFrederick the Third for short."

She leaned between the front seats and took Gulliver's snout in both her hands. "Gulliver J. McFrederick the Third. What a lovely name." One of her tears splashed onto Gully's nose. He didn't seem to mind. "This is my son Tyler, this is my daughter Lauren, and I'm Mrs."—she choked over a word I couldn't make out before trying again—"I'm Carolyn Rodriguez. Pleased to meet you all."

Mrs. Rodriguez kissed Gulliver on top of his nose. I gagged. "Bash, I think she's in shock."

"I don't have splints for shock. How about a broken arm? I can fix that."

The girl named Lauren studied her mom's face for a moment. Then she crawled into the backseat and hugged the hog. "Mom, he's warm. Maybe we should take him home."

Mrs. Rodriguez hugged Gulliver and sobbed some more. Lauren kept one arm around the pig and threw the other over the shoulders of her mother, who still twisted and stretched from front seat to back.

Weirdos. This whole neighborhood is full of weirdos. What these people needed—besides a life—was heat, and they sure weren't getting it out here stuck in a snow bank with the car doors open.

"Bash, we're closer to Jig and Jag's than your place. Let's take these people there." Nine-year-old twins Jig and Jag Gobnotter lived on the farm next door to Uncle Rollie's, meaning it was about a quarter mile away. We were almost there. "Mr. Gobnotter can come for the car with his tractor."

Lauren snuggled into Gulliver's blanketed back. "What's a Gobnotter?"

"It's their name. They have a fireplace."

"A fireplace." Lauren rubbed her mother's back. "Mom, don't worry. You'll be all right. I'll take care of you." The lady kissed the pig's snout again, then Lauren's. Her nose, I mean. Double yuck.

Lauren brushed black hair from her mom's forehead.

"Let me take Tyler to the fireplace long enough to warm him up." She turned teddy bear brown eyes on me. "Would they let us, Other Pig Boy?"

"Stop calling me that. I'm Raymond. Ray. Yes, they like company."

I took off my mittens and slipped them over Lauren's tanned fists so I could untie the sled and blanket from Gulliver. "Bash, quit looking for broken bones and help me bundle Tyler. He's freezing."

The lady still shook even though she'd stopped crying. "Uncle Al was friends with some Gobnotters. He'd talk about them when he came home from his hunting trips. My husband went with him a couple times." She chewed on her lip and rubbed the red of Tyler's cheeks. "Do you think they'd mind? Only for a minute so the kids can warm up. I'll stay to watch the car. Then we'll go."

Bash fumbled with Tyler's booster seat belt. "Go where? Your car's stuck." He winked at Tyler. "Mrs. G bakes great cookies. We'll call my ma from there. The church ladies will know where to find coats and boots and stuff."

The lady popped the car seat belt and lifted Tyler out. "Tell them we're Al and Carl Rodriguez's family." She bit back some sort of gurgle and whispered, "Carl." Gulliver nuzzled her nose with his snout. Gross.

Lauren's black hair bounced along her shoulders as she helped me slide the blanket from Gulliver. I patted one of Tyler's socked hands. "How old is he?"

"He's four, and I'm eleven. How old are you?"

"Twelve. Next month. Bash is only eleven, like you."

She untied the last knot and handed over the blanket. "Here you go, Other Pig Boy."

"Stop—" But Lauren already had rocketed back to the front seat.

I pulled the sled around to the other back door so we could reach Tyler.

Lauren wriggled beside her mother. "Mom, I'll send help right back. Or I'll come myself as soon as I get Tyler parked by the fireplace."

The lady nodded. Lauren leaped from the front door and nearly tumbled into the snow as she slipped and slid around the car. She loaded the boy onto the sled, sat down behind him, and wrapped Gully's blanket around both of them. "Mush!"

Bash and I pulled together, running the sled full of crash victims toward the Gobnotter farm.

Rescue Ranger Bash grunted. "Bummer. No broken bones. Why do we have to pull the sled?"

"Because Gulliver's keeping their mom company while she waits for the tractor. Now pull."

Tyler giggled and even Lauren laughed as we charged down the snow-clumped road. We nearly toppled the sled when we whipped into Jig and Jag's driveway. Tyler clapped. "Do it again, do it again!"

I unbundled Lauren and Tyler from the sled while Bash pounded on the back door. By the time I herded the kids toward the house, Mrs. Gobnotter bustled out and swept up Tyler. "You poor kids are chilled to the bone. Hurry, come in the house."

We left Mrs. Gobnotter, Jig and Jag fussing over the kids with blankets, soup, and toasted cheese sandwiches so we could ride with Mr. Gobnotter on his big ol' John Deere back to the stuck car. Gulliver and the woman both grinned at us from the front seat. "He only wanted out once. How did you housetrain him like that?"

Bash shrugged. "I didn't. You better check your seat again." The lady frowned as Bash ran behind the car with the other end of a chain hooked to the tractor.

A couple hours and a few mugs of hot chocolate later, Bash, Gulliver, and I hurried home, pulling the empty sled behind us. Bash's cheeks and nose were as red as I'd seen them—because I never saw his cheeks and nose in the cold.

"Where's your ski mask?"

"Aw, I gave my hat to Mrs. Rodriguez. You know grownups—they tell us to put hats on but never take one themselves."

"Oh."

"I've got a stocking cap. At home." Bash nodded toward my waist. "Why are your hands in your pockets?"

"Probably the same reason yours are."

"Gave your gloves to the people in the car?"

I shrugged. It turned into a shiver. I walked faster. Bash trotted to keep up. "You shouldn't be shivering like that just 'cause you're a kitten who lost his mittens. The sweatshirts Grandma gave us are warm."

"It was."

His eyebrows arched. "Was?"

"Lauren needed it," I mumbled.

"It was your favorite. You loved those swirls of colors."

"It was okay."

We were almost back to the farm. Gulliver, without his blanket, broke into a run. I'd have given him my scarf if I still had it. But I'd passed that to Lauren, and she'd wrapped it around Tyler. Twice.

Bash's teeth chattered. His nose reddened like a ripe strawberry. He dug his hands deeper into his pockets. "Tyler's got my sweatshirt."

I hunched into a run up the driveway. "Where's that family from? The Sahara Desert? They'd never seen real snow." My boots kicked wakes of the white stuff behind us. "Maybe they were camels in distress."

We ran Gulliver back to the pig pasture, where he sprinted for the warmth of his hutch. We sprinted for the warmth of the house. At the top of the porch steps, Bash turned his red nose to me. "You know the worst part, Ray-Ray?"

"What?"

"We never found any unconscious people with broken bones to rescue from avalanches. We don't get to check the fruit of goodness off our harvest basket list."

A kitchen gloved in wonderful warmth reached out and pulled us in. The furnace blower blasted hot air. The cheesy smell of macaroni mixed with hot dog chunks caused my belly to rumble. A tea kettle whistled on the stove. My glasses fogged, and the teeny icicles clinging to my eyelashes vaporized in teeny puffs of steam.

Bash slapped clumps of snow off his pants, interrupting my sighs. I tried to stomp circulation back into my toes. "Maybe in the summer we can try to find camels in distress."

Bash reached for a packet of hot chocolate and the teakettle. "We'll figure out goodness later. But I have a great idea for peace. We're gonna build a snow catapult."

I didn't want to know. But I'd find out. Ouch.

Chapter 8

Men Can Bake Hat Cookies Too

Aunt Tillie walked into the kitchen as we packed puffy marshmallows into mugs of steaming chocolate. She hugged us both. "Honestly, Sebastian, sometimes I don't know whether to laugh or scream."

Aunt Tillie moved to the stove to stir the macaroni and cheese. Bash flashed me a raised eyebrow that said, "What now?" I returned a quick shrug that said, "Who knows?"

Aunt Tillie pulled plates from a cupboard. "I just got off the phone with Mrs. Gobnotter, who told me all about it.

That was an idiotic, lunatic stunt harnessing that hog to a sled."

She plopped big helpings of macaroni and cheese with hot dog chunks onto the plates. "But then you found that poor Rodriguez family, up here from Florida without a stitch of winter clothing and no heat in that trailer."

Uncle Rollie tiptoed into the kitchen, shaking water from his freshly washed hands. He slipped up behind Aunt Tillie, wrapped his arms around her waist, and bunched up her apron to dry his hands. He kissed her ear.

Bash slid his hands to his neck to signal "I think I'm going to be sick."

I stuck out my tongue: "Blech. Me too."

Aunt Tillie turned in Uncle Rollie's tree-trunk arms and tapped him on the nose with the macaroni spoon, leaving a splotch of cheese behind. "Roland Hinglehobb, behave. There are children watching."

Uncle Rollie swiped the cheese off his nose, licked his finger, and chuckled. "They can find their own aprons. This one's mine."

Aunt Tillie pushed away and grinned. "It's *my* apron. You can dry your hands on the towels in the bathroom where you washed them."

"Great-granny's feather duster, Mattie, what fun is that?" Uncle Rollie always called her Mattie even though her name's Tillie. She calls him Roland. I don't know who Great-Granny Feather Duster is. Grownups are so weird.

Aunt Tillie jiggled a saucepan of peas on the stove and waved the macaroni spoon at us. "Boys, wash up for dinner."

After we said grace over the food, our forks flew. Macaroni and cheese with hot dog chunks is one of the greatest foods ever.

Uncle Rollie refastened a popped button on his red flannel shirt. "This meal's as good as apple, Mattie—it's a golden delicious."

I chased another forkful from my plate. "I thought the saying was 'good as gold.'"

Uncle Rollie winked. "It is. But have you ever cooked gold? Stuff's hard to chew."

Little Darla sat on a stack of catalogs. She banged her spoon on the table and clipped her macaroni bowl. Cheesy bits scattered across her face. "Good gold. Good gold."

I picked up my cup. Empty. The pitcher sat by Bash, which meant by Aunt Tillie's rules, I had to practice politeness. I sighed. "Pass the milk, please."

Bash grabbed the pitcher. "Plane, train, or subway?"

"What?"

Bash waved the pitcher over his head, then ducked it beneath the table. "Plane, train, or subway? Do you want me to hand it off high in the air like a flying plane, run it across the table like a train, or pass it to you under the table like a subway?"

Aunt Tillie's eyelid flicked. "Sebastian . . ."

"Or how about snowplow?" Bash clonked the pitcher onto the table and pushed, knocking salt and pepper shakers and the napkin holder out of the way.

Aunt Tillie's eyelid hopped. "Sebastian Nicholas Hinglehobb, this is a dinner table. Just hand the milk to Raymond."

"Sorry, Ma."

Uncle Rollie tugged his big, ol' handkerchief from his back pocket and spent several seconds wiping his mouth even though I didn't see any cheese drool. Aunt Tillie rubbed her temple. “Who taught you such a crude way to pass dishes at the table?”

Uncle Rollie rubbed his mouth so hard that he nearly choked on the handkerchief. Instead of jumping up to help his dad, Bash bobbed his head and snickered. Aunt Tillie dug harder at her temple. “Never mind. I know.”

Uncle Rollie coughed, wadded up the handkerchief, and stuffed it back into his pocket. “So, Gobby called after the boys showed up at their back door with a couple kids in tow. Ol’ Alfie Rodriguez was a good guy. I met his nephew Carl a few years back. Good kid.”

Aunt Tillie shook her head. “Too bad he had to go so soon. And with a young wife and two small kids.”

Bash passed me the peas by subway. “Lauren’s not so small. Beamer and I pulled her and her brother on the sled, and it wasn’t easy.”

“She’s smaller than I am.” I plopped peas onto my plate. “But yeah, she’s taller than Bash.”

“Not by that much. She probably was wearing high-heeled basketball shoes.”

Aunt Tillie’s eye flinched. “Boys. I meant they’re too young to lose their father. And what’s poor Carolyn—is that her name?—Carolyn Rodriguez going to do? We’re already calling neighbors to see what we can round up.”

Uncle Rollie nodded. “Good. Denny Dennison will be by on his snowmobile in a few minutes so we can go over to the Rodriguez trailer and figure out the furnace. Shouldn’t be hard. We’ll check the pipes and windows and such too.”

Bash gulped down a bite. “Can we go, Pops?”

“’Fraid not, son. Mr. Dennison’s dropping off Bonkers so you guys can play while we’re working.”

"Bonkers? Pops, that means all three of us can help. We'd have that furnace cooking so well, they could fry eggs on it. An' bacon an' homework papers, if they wanted to."

Uncle Rollie scratched his ear. "Yeah, that's what scares me. We'd sort of like it to warm the home, not melt it."

"So can we?"

"Nope. Not enough room on the snowmobile for both of us men, three boys, and our tools. Besides, one boy equals half a man, two boys equal half a boy, and three boys means no help at all."

Bash tilted his head. "Huh?"

I translated. "He thinks we'll goof off, get in the way, and forget to help."

Uncle Rollie *dinged* his finger in the air, like tapping an imaginary bell. "Give the boy a candy cane."

Bash sagged for a second, then brightened. "At least Bonkers will be here. Cool. Wait, we have candy canes left from Christmas?"

I gulped a drink of milk to keep from explaining his dad to Bash again.

Christopher "Bonkers" Dennison is Bash's neighbor from the other side of the woods and his best friend—besides me, I mean. Bonkers's dad takes care of injured wildlife for the state, and Bonk plans to be a veterinarian. He keeps a fleet of odd critters, including a pet skunk, and knows everything about all animals. Just ask him.

Other than being so smart, he's just as goofy as Bash.

We were in Bash's room when Bonkers burst through the door, cargo pants pockets bulging. "Look, guys, I brought my frogs." From each pocket, he pulled a two-inch tan frog colored with a black mask like a raccoon. "It's Sam and Ella."

Bash jumped up and took Sam. Or maybe Ella. "Way to go, Bonkers."

I poked my glasses up my nose. "Don't frogs hibernate in the winter?"

Bonkers nodded. "Mostly, yeah. Wood frogs like these guys actually go half frozen, including their brains."

Bash tapped Sam's head. Or maybe Ella's. "Frozen frog brains. Just like Beamer."

I rolled my eyes. "Ha, ha."

Bonkers handed me Ella. Or possibly Sam. Who could tell frogs apart?

"This is Ella. She's bigger than Sam."

Ella's puffy frog toes poked my fingers as she dug in. Bonkers cupped a hand over mine. "Don't let her jump. They go a long way. And they're hard to catch."

I held Ella up to my nose. She felt cool and smooth. A tan ridge line ran down either side of her back. Faded tiger stripes decorated her crazy-long back legs.

Bonkers took the frogs back and dropped them into his pockets. "I poured some damp dirt and wet leaves in my pockets so Sam and Ella would be comfortable."

That made sense. "So why aren't they frozen for the winter?"

"I missed them. I'm trying to wake them early by warming them up. So what are we doing today, guys?"

Bash dropped onto his bed. "I wanted to help fix the furnace. I wonder if they'll use dynamite to get it started. I could light dynamite. I'd be a good dynamite lighter."

"And that," I said, flopping onto my bed, "is why we're here instead of there."

Bonkers pulled out Bash's desk chair. "We don't have to play Candyland with Darla again, do we? She cheats."

"Nah. But Ma won't let us stuff her dolls in trucks and crash them down the stairs anymore, either."

Bonkers rested hands on chair and chin on hands. "That probably means we can't ride the sleds down the stairs again, either."

I popped up from my pillow. "You guys did what? Rode sleds *indoors*?"

Bash shrugged. "It was October. We were practicing for the snow."

Bonkers nodded. "It's way cool. You should try it—only, we can't, anymore."

I clunked my head against the wall. "Too bad we can't do anything to help Lauren and Tyler. If we were girls, we could bake cookies."

Bonkers sat up. "You don't have to be a girl to bake. My dad bakes all the time. Remember that pizza we had at my house? Dad baked it himself."

Bash jumped up. "Yeah. Pops says some of the best cooks in the world are guys." He paced in circles between the two beds and Bonkers's chair. "We could do it. It would be fruit."

I shook my head. "Not fruit. Cookies."

Bash paced faster. "No, fruit of the Spirit. We'll be doing good stuff. It'll count as fruit."

Bonkers peeked into his pockets to check on Sam and Ella. "Fruit of the Spirit. I remember those. Let's see, love, joy, peace, patience, uh . . ."

"Kindness," Cookie Baker Bash offered.

"Yeah, kindness, goodness, faith, um . . ."

My turn. "Self-control."

"Oh, yeah, self-control and gentleness. Which ones cover cookies?"

Bash shrugged. "Cookies are good so maybe goodness. Or kindness when we give cookies away. Who cares? We're gonna bake some fruit."

I tucked my pillow behind my head. "I don't like fruit in my cookies."

Cookie Baker Bash dashed from the room. We heard him crashing down the stairs, yelling all the way. "Ma, guess what? We're gonna bake cookies for Lauren and Tyler. We're gonna bake hat cookies."

Something clattered below. It sounded like the time I dropped a bunch of silverware in the kitchen. I didn't think Bash had made it there yet.

Bonkers looked at me. "Suppose we should go help?"

I stood. "Guess so. What are hat cookies?"

"Dunno. Maybe that's how you bake them."

"In a hat? Wouldn't the hat catch fire?"

Bonkers shrugged and headed out the door.

Chapter 9

Flying Cookie Dough and Leaping Frog Legs

Aunt Tillie's eye tic flapped at full throttle. "The three of you? Baking hat cookies? In my kitchen?"

When it came to Aunt Tillie's eye tic, one boy equaled hoisting the eyelid sail, two boys equaled revving the outboard motor, and three boys meant no eyelid anchor at all. She steadied herself against the back of a kitchen chair. A cluster of spoons, forks, and knives lay splattered at her feet.

Cookie Baker Bash paced the kitchen. "Yeah, we're gonna bake cookies. For Lauren, Tyler, and their mom. They need good stuff to eat. Boys can be bakers too."

Aunt Tillie's head bobbed as her eyes darted around the kitchen. "Well, I . . . that is . . . I just cleaned . . ." She started gathering spilt silverware. "Yes, it would be a good thing to do. I'm proud of you for thinking of it."

I kicked the back of Bash's sneaker. "I thought of it."

"No, you said it's too bad guys can't bake. I said we could."

Bonkers kicked the back of Bash's other sneaker. "I'm the one who said guys can bake."

Bash spun. "I'm the one who said yes. I'm the one who called hat cookies. I got to the kitchen first."

"But it wasn't your—"

"Boys!" Eye tics pinged Aunt Tillie's every word. "Stop arguing or nobody's baking any cookies. Whose idea it was doesn't matter. What matters is you want to help someone in need."

"Sorry, Ma."

"I'm sorry, Aunt Tillie."

"We didn't mean anything by it, Mrs. H. Can we bake cookies now?"

Aunt Tillie rubbed her temples. She dropped into the chair. Something whimpered, either the chair or Aunt Tillie. "Bring me the recipe box."

Bash pumped his fist. "Woo hoo." He shot across the kitchen, grabbed a green box from the counter, turned, and tripped. The box crashed to the floor. Note cards exploded everywhere. "Oops."

Aunt Tillie thumped her head onto the kitchen table. Her eyelid probably was beating a hole right through the placemat. "I'll sort them later. Hand me the hat cookies recipe when you find it."

"Here it is, Ma." Bash slapped a card in Aunt Tillie's palm. She pulled it into her lap and slid her head far enough off the table to read it. "Let's see, ungreased cookie sheets. Sugar, shortening, egg, vanilla, salt, flour, walnuts, milk, molasses, coconut . . ." She pushed away from the table. "Let's give this a try, though I don't know why."

Cookie Baker Bash yanked open a kitchen drawer. "Here's where Ma keeps her aprons. I'll take this one with the blueberries on it. Here ya go, Bonk, here's one with oranges. Beams, here's an apron with purple posies."

"Why do I have to wear an apron with flowers? Aren't there any with dump trucks or tractors or cows?"

Bash jammed the purple posies bib back into the drawer. "No trucks, but here's one with roses."

"Well . . ."

"And pink lace."

"No way."

"Boys, put on aprons, wash your hands with soap and water, and stop messing up that drawer, or the baking is off."

"Yes, Aunt Tillie." I dropped the roses-and-lace apron over my neck and tied the strings behind my back. "I'll get you for this, Bash."

The blueberries on Bash's apron bobbed as he laughed. Bonkers clamped a hand over his belly so tightly that he nearly squeezed juice from the oranges on his apron. *"Plbbbbt."*

Aunt Tillie twisted a knob on the oven. "Preheat to 350 degrees. Christopher, get the measuring cups from that drawer and measure out one cup of sugar. Sebastian, take one of those other cups and a spoon. *Carefully* pack a level cup of shortening."

Bonkers buried a yellow measuring cup into the sugar canister. Bash plopped gloppy white goo from the shortening tub into an orange measuring cup.

Aunt Tillie checked the recipe card. "Raymond, we need an egg, the box of salt, the bottle of vanilla, and the bag of flour."

I plucked a big brown chicken coop egg from the fridge and stuffed it into the pocket of my pink lace apron. At the pantry, I scooped up the salt with my left hand, popped the neck of the bottle of vanilla in my mouth to hold it, and threw my right arm around the five-pound bag of flour and yanked it off the shelf.

Never squeeze an open bag of flour.

A gusher of white powder *foofed* into my face. I coughed, gagged, and clawed at the flour. Both the salt box and flour bag plunged to the floor and burst open. The egg flew from my pink-laced pocket and smashed open in the middle of the mess. I spit out the bottle of vanilla. It landed, unbroken, in the pile of flour and salt.

Cookie Baker Bash slashed the shortening spoon at me. "Look, Ma, Beams mixed all the ingredients for us. We can sweep it up and put it in the bowl. Oops." A greasy glob of shortening flew from Bash's spoon and splashed down into the goo of the egg bleeding all over the salt and flour.

"I'll get it." Bash wrapped his fist around the gunky glob of shortening goo, which squished between his fingers like a fistful of Play-Doh. He jammed it into the measuring cup.

Bonkers swished the cup of sugar in the air. "Should I dump this on the egg? Do we need to pick the pieces of shell out first?"

"Stop."

Aunt Tillie stood in the middle of the kitchen, a tall, thin statue with hands clamped around clumps of hair nearly pulled from her head. Not even her eyelids twitched.

We froze. After a few seconds, the Aunt Tillie statue

gulped a couple quick breaths. Her voice whispered. "Matilda, you can do this."

Slowly, she looked around, staring each one of us straight in the eyes. "If you three hooligans want to bake in my kitchen, there will be no more running. No grabbing everything at once. No waving loaded spoons. You will follow directions. Is that clear?"

"Yeah, Ma. Sorry. I didn't mean to spill stuff in Beamer's gunk."

"Sorry, Aunt Tillie. It was an accident."

"Yes, ma'am, Mrs. H. Should I add the sugar now?"

"No dumping." Aunt Tillie's eyelid flickered. "You boys get the mop, broom, and washrags. Clean up. Now."

Ten or fifteen minutes later, we had the mess mostly swept up and wiped away. Bash scratched his head. A greasy group of hair soldiers stood at attention atop his noggin. "Baking's hard work."

Aunt Tillie peered at the recipe card. "Add the sugar gradually to the cup of shortening, stirring with that wooden spoon until creamy."

Bonkers tipped a slow stream of sugar into the bowl while the Basher ground the wooden spoon through the blob of shortening. "Phew. You need Superman muscles for this."

Aunt Tillie tapped the card. "Blend in the egg . . ."

I cracked a fresh egg against the bowl and dumped the guts over the creamy goo.

". . . a teaspoon of vanilla and a half teaspoon of salt."

Bonkers splashed a teaspoon of vanilla into the bowl. I scooped the salt onto the mix. Bash gripped both hands around the wooden spoon and rammed it through goo.

"Gradually add in two and a quarter cups of sifted flour, and mix thoroughly."

Bonkers tossed flour into a sifter and tried to set a world record cranking the handle. This time flour *foofed* into all our faces.

"*Christopher.* Sift, not spray."

After another cleanup delay, Cookie Baker Bash drove the spoon through the thick goop. A bead of sweat rolled off his forehead and dropped into the bowl. "Ma, how 'bout we use the electric mixer?"

Aunt Tillie's eyelid ticked off a couple beats. "Well, I suppose—"

"I'll get it." Bash dashed to the cupboard drawer, slammed two beaters into the mixer, and shoved them deep into the glop. The beaters *clunk-clunk-clunked* against the side of the bowl.

Another drop of sweat rolled off Bash's nose into the bowl. "Beamer, hand me that towel."

"What towel?"

"That one over there." Cookie Baker Bash pointed with the whirring mixer. *Zzzzwhhhhirrrrr.* Splatters of dough flew across the kitchen at about a hundred miles an hour.

Aunt Tillie threw her hands in front of her face. *"Turn it off. Turn it off!"*

Bash stilled the beast. "Sorry, Ma."

Daubs of cookie dough splotched everything—walls, tables, chairs, windows, and us. Bonk licked a finger. "Hmm. Needs more sugar."

A plop of dough dripped from the ceiling and landed in Aunt Tillie's hair. "Boys, I believe you know where the mop, broom, and rags are."

Twenty minutes later, Aunt Tillie set a smaller mixing bowl next to the splattered one. "Spoon about a third of that dough into this."

Bash reached for the blob of dough. Aunt Tillie snatched his hand. "With the spoon."

"Oh. Yeah."

The eye tic beat out a steady rhythm. "Christopher, stir a half cup of chopped walnuts and a tablespoon of milk into the small bowl."

She ran a finger across the lines written on the card. "Raymond, into the big bowl, stir a quarter cup of molasses and a cup of shredded coconut. With the spoon. No mixers."

I figured out why Bash sweated. My arms ached as I churned molasses and coconut through the sticky, gooey, gloppy wad of cookie dough. Years of making mud pies didn't prepare me for such thick goop. The oven heating at 350 degrees for the last hour didn't help. I wiped my sleeve across my forehead.

The phone rang in the living room. Aunt Tillie's eyes flicked from doorway to dough. "I'll be right back. Keep stirring, and don't do anything."

I held the spoon. "How can I keep stirring if I can't do anything?"

Cookie Baker Bash dug his fingers into the dough. "Let me taste. Hey, that's good. Cookie dough tastes better'n cookies."

Bonkers jumped over. "Let me try." And his hand went into the bowl as Bash reached for seconds. I licked the spoon. Not bad.

I wiped my forehead again. It was so hot that if there were any hibernating animals close by, they'd probably—

Something tan flew from one of Bonkers's pants pockets. A wood frog, wide awake in the warmth of the kitchen, plopped onto the counter. A second smooth, tan frog jumped beside it. One of them made *quacky-clicky* noises as its little throat quivered.

Sam and Ella had joined the party.

Bonkers dropped his dough and reached for the frogs. Sam—or possibly Ella—took a flying leap and landed smack in the middle of the brown cookie dough.

Bash's hand shot into the bowl, closing around frog and dough. He picked Ella—or possibly Sam—from the goop. "Should I lick the dough off of Sam's flippers? Will it give me warts?"

Bonkers slid Ella into one of his pockets. "Frogs don't give people warts. That's stupid. But you better not lick the cookie dough. You might accidentally swallow Sam. Frogs probably give heartburn."

Bash cleaned off the frog the best he could and handed Sam to Bonkers. "Quick, put him back in your pocket. Ma's coming."

Aunt Tillie walked in, phone in hand. "That's wonderful. Stop by on your way over. You can pick up cookies to take to them too. . . . Okay. . . . Bye-bye."

She clicked off the phone. "That was Mrs. Gobnotter. They've rounded up some winter clothes and Mr. Gobnotter is going to drive the stuff over to the trailer on his tractor. Now then, where were we?"

Bash raised his hand. "At the best part. Can I get the glass?"

"Is it that time already?" She looked at the recipe card. "Yes, I'm afraid it is. Yes, get one of your dad's tall milk glasses."

Bash ran to the cupboard. "Now you'll see why they're called hat cookies."

Aunt Tillie set the card down. "Raymond, from the big bowl, roll one-inch balls of dough and place them on the cookie sheet. Christopher, from the small bowl, roll half-inch balls of dough and place one on each of the brown dough balls—like a hat."

Bash smeared shortening on the bottom of the glass. "And I know my part. Grease the bottom of the glass, dip it in sugar, and smash the cookie snowmen until they're squishy flat."

Aunt Tillie's eye flickered. "You do not smash. You flatten to a quarter-inch thickness."

I rolled brown blobs. Bonkers rolled white globs. Cookie Baker Bash smashed the blobs and globs. Soon we had a sheet of flat brown cookies with white sugar hats.

Aunt Tillie picked up the first cookie sheet. "Now we bake for fourteen to sixteen minutes. Do the second sheet, boys. The recipe makes about four dozen cookies."

The kitchen filled with mouth-watering scents of coconut and molasses. We rolled and smashed cookies. We ate cookies. For some reason, we ended up with not quite two dozen.

Aunt Tillie blew a strand of floured hair from her forehead. "I guess we better mix up another batch." Then her eyelid flapped like crazy.

Mr. Gobnotter rumbled into the driveway on his big green tractor and picked up a couple dozen hat cookies for Lauren and Tyler and their mom, plus a few for himself, and headed for their mobile home.

Bash bit into another cookie. "It's our best fruit of the Spirit ever. Kindness is in the bag. I mean, basket."

I reached for two more cookies and dropped one in my pocket for later. "Cookies make great fruit."

When Uncle Rollie and Mr. Dennison stomped through the back door, kicking snow off their boots, Aunt Tillie served them a plate with coffee. Uncle Rollie grinned. "What kind did you make, boys? Frog cookies?"

I gulped. Cookie Baker Bash dug an elbow into my ribs. "Good one, Pops."

Uncle Rollie chewed. "Not bad. Blue tree frog, I'd say."

"Tan woo—" I caught another elbow. Bash took over the reply: "Nope, they're hat cookies. Made by men."

Uncle Rollie sipped his coffee. "Oh, the Rodriguez girl, what's her name, Lauren? She said to tell the Pig Boy and the Other Pig Boy that Tyler wants another sled ride, so hitch yourselves up and pull."

I wished that she'd stop calling me that.

"And she said there's a hole in your gloves. She's quite a card, that one. A strong helper too. Great with a wrench."

"Hey. We coulda done that, Pops."

"Then I wouldn't be eating hat cookies baked by men. I might be dumb, but I'm not stupid. Pass me another frog cookie."

"Plane, train, or subway, Pops?"

I downed another hat cookie myself. They really were good.

Bonkers slipped up beside us, patting one of his pockets. "Have you guys seen Ella?" he hissed.

I was going to be sick.

Chapter 10

The Snowball and Underwear Catapult

The wind's freezer breath slashed through our winter coats like sword-cicles. Even Bash's teeth chattered as we plowed our way to the chicken coop Wednesday morning. "Yesterday was so w-w-warm."

"It was thirty-five degrees." Frost formed on my words as they curled in smoky puffs out of my mouth. "Thirty-five means that instead of your whole body turning into a giant ice sculpture and shattering, just your fingers and toes will fall off from frostbite."

Bash tugged on his stocking cap—the replacement for the ski mask he gave to Mrs. Rodriguez—further over his ears and pushed his shovel straight toward the chicken coop. No snow swerves this morning. "That's what I said. Yesterday was warm. *Brrrr.*"

I crouched behind Bash, tucking my wool-capped head between his shoulder blades to duck another howl of bitter wind. We tumbled into the relative warmth of the chicken coop, where birds of a feather roosted together in feathery balls. I wondered if the roost would hold me too.

I clapped my mittens to see if I could feel my hands. Almost. "We ought to try hibernating through winter, like Sam and Ella wanted to do before Bonkers woke them. Ella was fast asleep when we found her behind the flour bag yesterday."

"Good plan. You've already got the frog face for it."

"Hey."

Bash grinned and dumped a few pellets into the feeders. I swished the broom without stirring up much gunk. I just wanted to get done and get to the cow barn and the warmth and sweet sterile smell of the milking parlor.

But I had to look. I couldn't help it. I peeked at the pen. Two folded gloves, just like yesterday. I didn't say anything.

I caught Bash looking. I braced myself for more heckling.

"Hey Beamer."

Here we go. "What?" I huffed.

"What do you get when you cross a chicken with a cow?"

I rolled my eyes. "A chicken with horns so she can cross the road?"

"Nope. Roost beef."

"Ugh. Can we go now?"

"Can't wait to use the wheelbarrow and clean up after the roost beef? Sure, looks like we're done here."

An hour or so later, after the cows were milked and pigs fed, Mighty Warrior Bash the Great paced a circle in the snow, sinking another inch with every packed-down lap. "Our snow catapult will be awesomeness itself."

"Let's go inside."

"We'll rain snowballs down on everyone even if they're miles away."

I hugged my arms and hopped. "The milk's in the tank, the barns and pens clean, and the animals are fed. There's no reason to freeze to death."

"Nobody will be able to sneak up on Mighty Warrior Bash the Great and Foot Soldier Beamer. And then we'll harvest the fruit of peace for our fruit of the Spirit basket."

"I can't feel my feet. I think they fell off."

Mighty Warrior Bash stopped pacing. "It's warm now. I looked at Pops's speedometer on the barn. It's going almost thirty-five miles per hour."

"Thermometer. And they're called degrees. Thirty-five's still like Antarctica."

"Never been there. 'Sides, we'll do the first part of building a snow catapult inside."

"Oh."

"Let's see, first we'll need Ma's bicycle. And some of Pops's tools."

"Uh, oh."

"C'mon, everything we need's in the garage. It'll be splendiferous."

I shivered, followed Bash into the garage, and closed the door. He wheeled a sparkly green bicycle out of a mess of bikes in a back corner. “Excellent. Two big inner tubes.”

Bash sifted through a toolbox on the workbench. “Ray-Ray, dig out one of the old milking pails from behind Pops’s camping stuff.”

I wound my way between an air compressor and some broken chairs, over a couple wagons, and around pieces of an old corn picker to get to the camping gear. I clawed aside three folded camping chairs, a couple tent bags, a rolled-up pink, purple, and orange paisley sleeping bag—

I hoisted the sleeping bag. “This thing’s so scary it would keep you awake.”

Bash snickered. “And it gives you nightmares when you do fall asleep. Pops picked it up at an auction sale somewhere as a joke. Never saw another one like it. Find the milk pail yet?”

I dumped the ugly sleeping bag and sifted through a camp stove, frying pans, water bottles, and other gunk. When I pulled aside a couple piles of plastic tarps, I found a stack of banged-up stainless steel buckets underneath. “Found them.”

“Cool.”

I tugged a bucket off the stack, threw the camping gear back on top, and zig-zagged back across the garage. Bash spun a wrench around a wheel hub of the bicycle. I dropped the bucket and watched. “Um, won’t your mom be angry?”

“Nah. She can’t ride through snow. When it melts, we’ll put the tires back.” Bash pried the front tire off the wheel, plucked out the inner tube, and handed it to me. “Squeeze the rest of the air out, Beamer. We need ’em flat, like giant rubber bands.”

We flattened both inner tubes against the cold concrete floor, pressing the last gasps of cold breath from them, sort of like squeezing an almost empty tube of toothpaste. Then we screwed the caps back onto the valve stems. "That shows we're responsible with Ma's things."

Bash pulled a knot of rawhide bootlaces from his pocket. "C'mon, Beamer. It's time for super snowballing."

Frosty air billowed through the flapping door he left open behind him. I sighed, rewrapped the scarf around my nose and mouth, tugged the knit cap further down over my ears, and trudged toward winter.

I found Bash tying the milk bucket between the two stretchy inner tubes, and tying the inner tubes to a couple of skinny, wobbly black-and-white birch trees near the road. The little trees stood a couple feet apart. Soon the pail on inner tubes dangled between the two birches.

"It's a giant slingshot."

I shrugged. "I don't get it."

"You pack a bunch of snow into the bucket, like this, then grab the bucket and pull it back as far as you can, like this . . ."

Mighty Warrior Bash the Great walked backward, straining on the last few steps as the skinny birches bent. Bash touched the bucket nearly to the ground. ". . . then you let go—*like this*."

The old pail rocketed from his hands and sprang skyward. It *thwanged* between the birches, which swished forward like long, leafless arms waving good-bye. The bucket *whumped* to a stop at the other end of the rubber band inner tubes, spun crazily, and jingled and jangled between the two trees. Just before it stopped shimmering, snow slipped from the pail and plopped to the ground. A snow bucket castle slouched between the birches.

"Mighty Warrior Bash the Great *Goof*." I whooped. "We'll be able to defend ourselves against snow ants, provided they wait between the trees."

Bash gnawed on his tongue. It looked like he chewed on a golf ball as he turned the bucket in his gloves. The mighty warrior—felled by bicycle inner tubes and a water bucket.

Suddenly, Bash dropped the bucket. I saw fire in his eyes. *Oh, man, his brain overheated. He's going to say something crazy weird now.*

"We'll use your underwear."

Chapter 11

Snowbombs Away!

I knew he'd say something crazy weird.

I grabbed my belt loops and hung on. "Not on your life, buddy boy. Use your own shorts."

"Not the ones you have on. I mean those weird Abominable Snowman undershorts back in the room. They're perfect."

"No, they're not!"

Bash bolted toward the house. "Be right back."

Five minutes later, my Bumble the Abominable Snowman shorts swung between the inner tubes in place of the dented milk bucket.

"See, your shorts make the perfect payload pouch for our super slingshot."

"Take them down. It's embarrassing."

"That an eleven-year-old kid has snowman underwear? Yep. But watch this." Bash packed a heavy, wet snow cannonball right over Bumble's face. Holding the boxers wrapped around the snowball, Bash backed up as far as a little kid without much muscle could.

He let go. My shorts snapped heavenward.

The giant snowball arced gracefully through the cold sky. The thin birch trees—the forks of the biggest slingshot I'd ever seen—swished and shuddered, waving good-bye to the rocketing snowball. The snow cannonball sailed, landing with a *whump* about half a football field away.

It was majestic.

I said what any kid whose underwear danced between two trees would say: "They're my shorts. I get the next turn."

I thumped together a super snowball, packing it as tightly as possible so it wouldn't break up in flight. I loaded the ammo into the seat of my pants—the ones I wasn't wearing—and stretched the inner tubes back as far as I could.

I let go.

Whoosh. The makeshift slingshot hurled the super snowball through the air. *Whump.* "Ha! Sixty yards, at least. Probably seventy. Beat that."

I nearly forgot that it was cold as Bash and I took turns sailing snowballs across the yard. We sailed them over fences, sheds, and fields, perfecting our packing and aiming.

Bash congratulated himself as a mighty warrior. "This gets the fruit of peace, for sure. Nobody, not even a kid from the next county, would dare start a war against us. Oh, yeah. They won't bother us."

The warrior gazed across the snowdrift horizon. "Now if only we had a kid from the next county to battle."

Then I saw them.

Way down the road, a figure bundled in a pink snowmobile suit pulled a sled. Someone else who looked like a wilted flower drooped along beside the pink person.

The kid in pink had to be Bash's pesky neighbor, Mary Jane Morris. With the blizzard blocking roads to the city, Mary Jane made deliveries from her family's Morris's Corner Store and Seed Emporium to the closer farms while her dad zoomed to some of the further ones, towing a wagon behind his snowmobile. Already thirteen, Mary Jane Morris sported chocolate curls, laser blue eyes, and two of the scariest fists ever to smash my shoulders.

I didn't recognize the wilted flower, but I could guess. Lauren Rodriguez. Mary Jane probably had all kinds of winter clothes she'd outgrown that would fit Lauren. Plus, Mary Jane stalked around doing good deeds all the time when she wasn't too busy clobbering Bash for his.

I squinted at the approaching girls. I turned to the undershorts slingshot in the trees. *Bash wouldn't. Would he?*

Bash followed my gaze. He whispered. "Mary Jane."

Mighty Warrior Bash the Great snapped to attention. "Foot Soldier Beamer, prepare to tie the catapult to trees by the road."

"No way. Mary Jane'll pulverize us. And she'll see my underwear!"

Mighty Warrior Bash ignored me as he dismantled the catapult, scouted for two snappy trees near the road, and retied it. "Help me pack snowballs, Private."

I handed Bash a snowball. "You're crazy."

With a mighty *thwang*, the round, white missile arced skyward from the Abominable Snowman shorts, then dropped in a crumbling mist about twenty or thirty yards in front of Mary Jane. *Whump*.

The pink bundle stopped. I couldn't see them at this distance, but I felt those icy blue eyes sizing me up for a bruising. The wilted flower perked up as if somebody had watered it.

Mighty Warrior Bash the Great scooped up more snow. "Reload! Reload!"

Thwang.

Whump. To the right and way short.

"Again!" the Warrior cried.

The pink bundle stomped through the snow, approaching our gunnery. The flower flounced alongside, grinning.

Thwang. Whump. Left and short.

The pink bundle stormed on, white boots churning through white snow. The flower scooped up some snow, packed it, and threw. She was too far away, but still it wasn't a bad throw. For a girl. I wished I could throw like that. But we had a snowball catapult.

Thwang. Whump. Way to the left.

"Reload! Reload!" I sensed panic in the Warrior's voice. Or maybe that was me.

The pink bundle was close enough now that I could see the glare of her eyes and the groceries poking out of the bags and boxes on her sled. The braying voice chilled me.

"Sebastian Nicholas Hinglehobb. Raymond William Boxby. If a snowball so much as touches me . . ."

Thwang. Whump. To the right and short. Again. Practice made the Warrior worse. The flower giggled and heaved another snowball that nearly covered the distance. The kid had an arm on her like a, well, a snow catapult in hand-me-downs.

Bash dug frantically into the snow. "Beamer, more snowballs. Quick. Before they get here."

Thwang. Whump.

The oncoming Mary Jane hooted. "Keep aiming at me, and I'm as safe as can be. Losers."

Suddenly, she stopped. She leaned forward and rubbed her eyes. "Is that . . . underwear?"

She didn't have to yell.

Lauren exploded in laughter. "It's . . . it's . . . it's the Abominable . . . *snort* . . . Snowman. On little boy boxers."

Mary Jane dug fists into her hips. "You're throwing snowballs at me with your underwear?" I bet all the neighbors could hear her now. "Which one of you wing nut dweebs still wears cartoon underwear?"

Lauren nearly fell over laughing. Bash started to point a gloved finger at me, but I shoved him aside. "Gimme that snowball." I thumped it a few more times to pack it tight, fitted it over Bumble's face and practically ran backward. Bash wrapped his arms around my waist and hauled me back three more steps. The treetops nearly touched the snow.

I let go.

Thwaaaannngggggg.

We tumbled backward, spilling into a pile of snow. The snowball sailed high. Mary Jane stared at the long, long flight. Slowly, lazily, it hurtled downward right toward . . .

Oh, no.

Bash clambered to his feet, digging his boots into my back like a sprinter at the starting blocks. Mary Jane's mouth dropped wide open. Silently, I wished her out of the way: *Run, MJ, run. Away, I mean.*

She didn't move.

Ka-pow.

In a spray of mushy white plumes, the snowball bloomed like a cloud atop Mary Jane's hood-covered head. A plump cloud, exploding as if it had been shot from, well, inner tubes, underwear, and trees.

Mary Jane fell, a puffy, pink tree toppling backward atop her sled full of food.

Ker-splat.

Streams of milk and orange juice squirted like fountains from crushed cartons. A plastic bread bag whooshed open, firing slices across the snow like a deck of whole-wheat playing cards. Showers of green beans, flour, sugar, and corn rained down upon Mary Jane. Squishes of eggs, bananas, and grapes mushed up her sides. The splatters decorated her pink snowsuit in every color found on grocery shelves.

Then all was still. Lauren knelt over Mary Jane and brushed away food bits, and pieces, and chunks. She leaned close and tilted her head as if listening for something. Lauren picked up a fallen doughnut, bit into it, stood, shook her head at us while chewing, and backed away from the sled.

I held my breath. "Do you think she's hurt?"

A second later, like terror rising from mist, Mary Jane sat up. I felt the frosted frigidness of blazing blue eyes. Bash gulped. "Nope. But we're gonna be. *Run!*"

Chapter 12

Beamer and the Chicken-Hatted

"Told ya we'd harvest fruit today. We got vegetables too."

I jammed another tub of snow-covered cottage cheese into a torn grocery sack and glared at the Basher. "Go chew a smashed egg carton."

Bash dug a bag of potatoes from beneath Mary Jane's sled and dumped them in a tattered cardboard box. "But Beamer, we did it. We're farmin' the fruit of the Spirit."

"How do you figure that, genius?"

"When we promised to pay for the groceries with our Christmas money and deliver them for her—"

"So she'd stop whapping us with my underwear."

"—Mary Jane stopped beating you up—"

"*Us*. Both of us. At once."

"—and you stopped squealing."

"Both of us. At once."

"And we made peace with her. See, Beamer. We did it. The fruit of peace. I told you. Check it off the list."

I stared at my cousin. "Do you do anything with your head but use it to park your hat?" I rammed a half-full loaf of bread into another bag. If this was peace, gentleness would break my legs.

"Hurry it up," Mary Jane barked. "You have a lot of groceries to deliver."

Lauren muffled giggles behind a floppy mitten. "That was an awesome cool catapult, Other Pig Boy. Wish I could have fired it off. Too bad it fell apart."

I tossed a crinkled grocery bag onto the sled. "I'm Beam—Ray. My name's Ray. And the catapult didn't *fall* apart. Mary Jane ripped it apart. And whapped us with my . . . whapped us with it." Even through the cold, I felt heat flushing my cheeks.

Lauren giggled again. "I know. That looked like fun too." She spun away and grabbed Mary Jane's arm. "Thanks." Mary Jane smiled at Lauren.

Bash shook a bent egg carton, dumping shell crumbs and goo into the snow. "Too bad Beamer already collected our eggs this morning. We could replace this from our chicken coop."

"You collected the eggs. It was your turn."

"Nope, I didn't do it. You were 'sposed to."

"No way, Buster Butterbean. I gathered eggs the last three mornings, and the last three nights."

Bash flipped the empty, messy egg carton into a box. "I don't think so. Otherwise—"

"Zip it." Mary Jane stood with arms folded, boot tapping, her posture matching her teacher voice. The smile was gone. "Obviously, neither one of you clowns collected eggs. So let's go get them now, shall we?"

Bash ducked his head. "Sure thing, Mary Jane."

Bash and I pulled Mary Jane's grocery sled to the farm and toward the chicken coop. We fished out three empty egg cartons and tromped into the chicken coop. Lauren gasped. "Oh, wow. Can I hold one?"

I skipped out of the way of Mrs. Beakbokbok's beak. "Not a good idea, Lauren. Chickens are mean."

She didn't hear me. She was too busy cuddling a feathery ball of black-and-white speckles.

Bash scratched the hen's head next to its red comb. "This is Cheryl Checkers P. Featherchucker."

Lauren's lip trembled. A tear splashed into speckled feathers. Lauren hugged the bird. "Daddy."

I tapped her on the shoulder. "Um, it's a hen. You're thinking of roosters."

Lauren's eyes snapped at me. "Not the chicken. *My* Daddy. Daddy loved animals. We spent hours in the barnyard exhibit at the zoo. Daddy scratched behind cows' ears, combed the ponies' manes, fed the goats. He liked chickens best. All the colors, the way they walked, even the dumb noises they made . . ."

Lauren sniffled, quivered, and buried her face into Cheryl's back. "Daddy."

My eyebrows arched a question at Bash. His shoulders shrugged, "Don't ask me." He scraped a toe through a clump of straw on the floor. I gulped. Now what?

Mary Jane knelt and tucked a big white hen into her arms. She sidled up to Lauren until their shoulders touched. For a moment the girls just stood there, Lauren shaking with her face buried in a bird's back, Mary Jane locked at her side, cuddling a hen.

"This white one is called a leghorn," Mary Jane whispered to no one in particular.

Bash brightened. "Her name is Lizzie Longhorn Leghorn. I named her myself."

Mary Jane ran a finger around the red comb flopping atop Lizzie's head, down to the red wattles flapping beneath Lizzie's yellow beak. If the bird could have, it would have purred.

"Why did the chicken cross the playground?" Bash asked. "To get to the other slide!"

Lauren snuffled into the chicken down. Mary Jane smoothed Lizzie's feathers. I tried to figure out if it was safe to breathe. Bash looked perplexed. "The other slide. Get it? See, the chicken crossed the road to get to the other side, so she crossed the playground to get to the other slide." He scratched his head and walked away.

Mary Jane kept whispering. "Leghorns like this one lay big, white eggs." Mary Jane tilted her head until it rested against Lauren's. "The speckled hen you're holding is called a Plymouth Rock chicken. Plymouth Rock hens lay big brownish pinkish eggs."

The girls stood quietly shoulder-to-shoulder, head-to-head, hugging chickens. After a few seconds, Mary Jane leaned forward and kissed the leghorn's head. "Aren't they sweethearts?"

I rolled my eyes and stepped away from another attack by Mrs. Beakbokbok. She was *not* a sweetheart. I bumped into the roost. A familiar flurry of flapping whumped overhead. A downdraft swirled. Plop. Eight claws dug toeholds through my woolen hat.

"Not again." I swished mittened hands at the butterball using my head as an egg.

Lauren laughed.

I froze in mid-swish. She quivered, but this time in gales of giggles, and gurgles, and girly gulps. Cheryl Checkers flapped in her arms as if applauding some big joke. And I knew the name of the big joke—me.

The bird on my head slid toward my left ear, taking my hat with her. With a fluster of flapping, the bird ran back up to the top of my head and dug in through another section of wool. Lauren doubled over, squealing and hooting. Cheryl Checkers and Lizzie Longhorn cackled, and even Mary Jane snickered, her blue eyes dancing.

I reached for the bird. "S'not funny."

Lauren caught her breath. "Daddy tried for years to get a chicken to sit on his head. I never saw one actually do it until now." And she dissolved into another round of sniggers and snickles.

Mary Jane burbled. "That's a Rhode Island red. They lay brown eggs. I believe I've heard Sebastian call her Queen Clucken Henny Penny of Red Rhodes."

"What a silly name." Lauren hugged Cheryl Checkers. "Let her stay on your head, Other Pig Boy."

Mary Jane steadied a slip-sliding Henny Penny. So quietly that I almost missed it, she breathed into my ear, "Thank you, Raymond." For what, I had no clue.

I grimaced and picked up the egg basket. With girls giggling behind me, one hen sitting and sliding atop my head, and another hen nipping at my toes, I began gathering eggs.

Lauren skipped to my side. "Let me help." She cuddled the hen into the crook of her left arm and plucked eggs from nesting boxes with her right. She jumped when her hand came back full of a big, green egg. "Ew, is it rotten?"

"Naw. It's supposed to be green. See that brown bird pecking at my boots? It's called an Easter-egger hen."

"So that's how you get green eggs for the ham?"

I pulled a tan egg from the next box and added it to the basket. "Just the shells are green, not the insides."

Lauren rolled the egg around her mitten before placing it in the basket. She squatted to pet Mrs. Beakbokbok, who, of course, nestled into Lauren's mitten. "Do they have any other Easter-egg hens?"

"That white and butterscotch one over there with the white feather beard lays blue eggs. Bash calls her Polly Pufflecheeks Piffles."

"Cool."

"I guess. The rest of the flock is normal. Normal for chickens."

Lauren stood. "Hey, if a rooster sitting on the peak of the chicken coop lays an egg, on which side would the egg roll?"

"Neither."

Lauren grinned. "Can't fool you, Other Pig Boy."

"I was up on the roof. There's so much snow up there that the rooster's egg would just sit there."

If Lauren had been drinking milk, it would have shot out her nose. "Roosters don't lay eggs."

"Huh? Oh. Yeah. That too." C'mon, it's hard to think with a chicken squatting on your head.

Lauren set another egg, a tan one, in the basket. "What's up with Pig Boy?"

Bash rubbed his chin like a kid trying to choose between pizza with pepperoni and pizza with sausage. Except his narrowed eyes studied the storage pen, not a pizza.

Mary Jane laid a hand on Bash's shoulder. "Sebastian, what's wrong?"

"The gloves. They're gone."

Chapter 13

The Angel without Knowing It

Mary Jane turned Bash around. "What gloves?"

"Three days ago there were no gloves in that pen. Two days ago, there was one."

Aha! So he knew I was right. I started to nod, but the bird on my head slipped. She dug in new toeholds. "Ow."

Bash scratched his ear. "Yesterday, there were two, folded on that far feed sack. They were still there this morning. Now they're not."

Bash flipped the latch and stepped into the pen. Mary Jane tip-toed behind him. "What kind of gloves?"

Bash sifted through the straw with his boot and tugged aside feed sacks. "Gloves. Blue, fuzzy ones. The kind that clumps of snow stick to. Rotten for snowballs. I wouldn't have any like 'em."

Mary Jane peered around burlap sacks and into the corners of the pen. "I do. That is, I used to. I couldn't find them today when I was sharing my winter clothes with Lauren."

Lauren held a tan egg with brown speckles. She set Cheryl Checkers onto the floor and took the egg to Mary Jane. "Look at this one."

Mary Jane rolled the egg in her gloved hand before fixing Bash in a blue-eyed stare. "Sebastian Nicholas Hinglehobb, is this your idea of a joke?"

Bash shook his head. "It's not a yoke. It's the whole egg."

"My fuzzy blue gloves weren't in our back breezeway. But we found two speckled eggs just like this in the box of spare gloves. This is one of your pranks."

Bash held up his hands. "I don't walk that far to pull a gag. Not until April Fool's Day."

"How about your freakazoid friends, Christopher Joseph Dennison or Jehoshaphat Isaac Gobnotter?"

"Nope. Bonkers was over to bake cookies yesterday. He didn't come into the chicken coop. Last I saw Jig was when we rescued Lauren and Tyler and their ma. That was at his house."

Mary Jane peered at the egg, then at Bash. She handed the egg back to Lauren, who passed it to me for the basket. "So how did my mittens get to the chicken coop? And where are they now? And how did your eggs get to my house?"

I wriggled beneath the weight of my chicken hat. "The Easter bunny?"

Lauren stifled a snicker. Bash paced a slow circle around us. "We don't know they were your gloves 'cause they're not here."

He paced another circle. "Where'd they go?"

I shrugged. "The chickens ate them so they could lay balls of yarn?"

Lauren giggled. It reminded me of the brook waterfalls in spring. It sure beat crying. Bash ignored it all and paced faster. "I've got it. Somebody took them."

Mary Jane rolled her eyes. "Well, of course somebody took them. Otherwise, they'd still be here. If it wasn't the other kids, how about your parents?"

Bash shook his head. "Ma's been in the house all day. After he finished milkin', Pops holed up in the machinery barn. He's rebuilding the corn planter for spring."

Mary Jane nodded. "So it was somebody cold who needed gloves."

Bash screeched to a halt. "I know who."

"Who?"

"An Angel Without Knowing It."

Mary Jane stammered. "You're blaming an angel for stealing gloves?"

"'Member our Sunday school memory verse from three weeks ago? Um, 'Let brotherly love continue. Don't neglect to show hospi . . . hospi . . .' um, to be nice, 'cause—how's it go? Oh, yeah—'for by doing this some have welcomed angels as guests without knowing it.'"

Bash could remember more Bible memory verses than any kid I knew. He got most of the words right too. I was trying to work my way up to memory verse champion, but it was hard. I closed my eyes. "Um, was that the one in Hebrews?"

"Yep. Chapter thirteen."

"That doesn't make sense." I poked at my glasses. Henny Penny slid to the side again and flapped her way back to the top of my head. Several red feathers floated around me.

Bash caught one of the floating feathers to use as a pointer stick. "Sure it does. If the angel came out in the open wearing white robes and six wings sprouting from his back, we'd know it. But he comes to the chicken coop. It already has feathers, so we won't notice. He's in his Angel Without Knowing It secret agent disguise."

I chewed on that for a second as I placed eggs from the basket into the banged-up cartons. "Maybe. So that would mean Mary Jane showed brotherly love with her gloves."

"We helped. It's our chicken coop."

Mary Jane stomped her boot. "No, no, no, no. Why would an angel need gloves? Or hide in a chicken coop?"

"'Cause Beamer and I are collecting fruit of the Spirit."

"Excuse me?"

"Fruit of the Spirit. From Galatians. Love, joy, peace, patience, kindness, goodness, faith, gentleness, and self-control."

"And that leads to angels how?"

Bash waved the chicken feather. "It had to be somebody who knew we were collecting fruit. So he knew we'd do good deeds."

I shook my head. The chicken hat skittered. "What about the footprints in the snow? Why would an angel leave footprints?"

Mary Jane huffed. "Of course there were footprints in the snow. You left them this morning. Ours are there now."

Bash pointed the feather at her. "But were there other footprints?"

She threw up her hands. "How should I know? I wasn't watching for footprints."

"See, it was an Angel Without Knowing It. I know it. He came to help us harvest the fruit of kindness by letting us give him gloves to warm his cold hands."

I looked up from the cartons. "Except he had to bring his own gloves."

Mary Jane crossed her arms across her pink snowmobile suit. "You're hopeless, Sebastian Nicholas Hinglehobb."

I held up the last egg carton. Two white eggs, one brown, one tan, and one green. Seven of the dozen spots remained empty. "We don't have enough eggs again. They're gone with the gloves."

Bash scratched his ear. "Angels eat eggs? Who knew?"

Mary Jane turned to the door. "I think, boys, you better get moving. You have a lot of groceries to deliver."

I lifted Henny Penny from my head and placed her on the roost. It felt good to get that load off my mind.

Bash rubbed his chin. Finally, he yanked off his green wool hat and tossed it inside. "For the Angel Without Knowing It."

We trooped back outside. Lauren paused at the door and waved at the chickens. "Bye, Daddy. I love you."

"They're—" was the only word I got out before Mary Jane nudged me with her elbow. I closed my mouth. Lauren spun and sped past me out the door. Mary Jane hurried after her.

I surveyed the three dozen feather balls strutting and clucking inside. "They're chickens. Just chickens."

I slammed the door and took off. For the first time, I welcomed the ice cream breath of outdoors on my face. The chicken coop creeped me out.

And I knew we'd have to go back.

Chapter 14

Of Mice and Muffs

The next morning Bash shoveled a straight line to the chicken coop and ran inside. Before I made it to the door, he blocked the entrance. “It’s gone, Beamer. My hat’s gone.”

I brushed past him. “Where?”

I hurried to the chicken wire pen. No hat. Not on the floor. Not on the feed sacks. Not anywhere. No gloves, either. I backed away, picked up the broom, looked around the chicken coop, and set the broom aside.

“Maybe a mouse took it. You should leave one of the cats in the chicken coop.”

“Mrs. Finley Q. Ruffeather Beakbokbok chases ’em off.”

I danced out of Mrs. Beakbokbok's way while steering clear of the roost. "Imagine that."

Bash unlatched the gate, dropped to his knees, and scooted around the pen. "Don't see any mouse holes. And the chickens can't get in."

"It's a mouse." I counted eggs. "A hungry one. We're seven short again."

"You're sure?"

"I can count. And see. No blue egg. No green egg."

Bash wandered over and sifted through the egg basket. "Hmm." He grabbed handfuls of straw, checked nesting boxes for bedding, and put the straw back. "They'll probably make up for it tonight."

"The evening collections run short too." I straightened a tuft of fluffed straw in one of the nesting boxes. "Looks like we're done. Might as well go help with the milking."

Bash stared at the hatless, gloveless pen, and scratched his ear. He unzipped his coat a few inches, reached inside and came up with a plastic grocery bag. From inside the bag, he pulled out big, puffy red earmuffs on an oversized plastic band. He set the red muffs in the center of the pen, latched the gate, wadded up the plastic bag, and zipped it back inside his coat.

"Mice can't drag those things through any mouse hole."

"Aha! You think it's mice too."

"Nope. But it might be a rat. A big one. And her name is Mary Jane."

I checked the chickens' feed trough. Full. "Why would Mary Jane steal gloves, eggs, and a hat?"

"Because she's a rat. Did you notice how she wanted to blame Jig or Bonkers? That got me to thinkin'."

"You shouldn't do that."

Bash paced. "If Mary Jane is so eager to blame it on the guys, maybe it's so I wouldn't suspect the girls."

"So you're giving her earmuffs?"

Bash grinned. "Let's just say I set a rat trap. C'mon, let's get to the barn."

I tucked my scarf around my face. "It's mice, Bash. You'll see."

Bash studied the muffs. "Yep. You'll see."

Bonkers Dennison clambered over one of the five-foot-tall snowdrifts in the backyard. "A snow cave. This will be awesome. Thanks for calling, Bash."

Even though the last cow pie was shoveled and the last hog slopped, for some insane reason, we remained out in the cold. Bash's bird-brainstorm of tunneling a snow cave into one of the super snowdrifts was the insane reason.

I jumped up, trying to peer over the drift. "You guys are nuts. No, you're icicles. Icicles shaped like nuts, that's what you are."

Bash, pink face blooming red, turned to Bonkers. "You know we gotta do it for his own good, Bonk."

Bonkers, brown face glowing against the bristling snow, nodded. "Yep. City kids from the South got to learn."

I climbed up the bank to join the frozen frog brains. "Virginia Beach isn't that far south. We get some snow there, too, you know. Besides, we moved to Ohio in September, remember?"

"Yeah, in town." Bash and Bonkers charged, each

thumping one of my shoulders. *Splat.* I landed flat on my back, sinking three or four inches.

"Hey! Get me up." I thrashed and scrambled, flipped, sank deeper, kicked and clawed until I wobbled to my feet, my face full of fire, my boots full of ice. Well, snow.

Bash and Bonkers doubled over laughing, whomping each other on the back as they hooted. "Look, Southern boy tried to make a snow angel."

"More like a snow chicken."

"A snow chicken with warts and wrinkles and knobby knees."

"An' it exploded. Like a giant burp. Beamer sure made a mess of that snow."

I leaped, arms wide, smashing into two padded icicle numbskulls, tackling both dummies at once. All three of us plopped into a heap. We rolled around, shoving mittens of snow into each other's noses. The fresh snow billowed around us, sprinkling us until we looked like puffy powdered doughnuts.

"Stop!" Bash yelled between chortles. Bonkers swatted another spray of snow at both of us and fell back laughing. Even I felt warmer and grinned. Just a little warmer. Just a little grin. Bash sat up and let a scoop of snow flutter from his mitten. "Not good packin' snow on top."

I licked flakes off my lips and readjusted the scarf over my face. "What's the difference?"

Bonkers swished arms and legs to make a snow angel. "See, this new stuff that came down last night's too fluttery. Too cold. The good carvin' and buildin' snow is underneath."

I dug my gloves into the snow and tried to crunch it into a ball. It didn't stick nearly as well as yesterday's catapult snowballs. I held today's snowball in my palm. The ball cracked down the middle and fell apart. "So we're going to burrow like chipmunks into the snow. We're going to pack ourselves in ice?"

"Yep. We're gonna be Secret Agent Snowmunks."

Bonkers jumped up. "We're the snowmunks of the secret tunnels."

I brushed snow from my pants before it could soak through to the second pair I wore underneath them. And the long johns beneath that. "What secret tunnels?"

Bash pointed. "We're not going to dig down. We're going to the wall of a snowdrift and tunnel in. C'mon, I know the perfect drift where we can start digging our secret hideout."

Bonkers ran after Bash. "Let's mark the tunnels this time so we don't get lost like last year."

"Wait. First, let's call all the kids to help. We can carve the best secret hideout ever."

I held up my mitten. "You mean we're going to tunnel through there. Into the snow? Aren't your brains frozen enough?"

"It's cold out here. But inside there"—Bash poked the wall of the snowdrift—"it's warm."

Bonkers nodded. "Yep. It's like an igloo. Snow makes great insulation."

Bash plunged a fist into the snow bank. "'Sides, we always sweat when we dig. You'll be toasty."

Another gust of wind about knocked me over. I shivered. And sighed. "Whatever. Let's just get out of this wind."

"Cool!"

"Did you have to use that word?" I chased after Bash and Bonkers as they headed for the phone to call the rest of the gang. Actually, carving out a series of secret tunnels could be kind of fun. Too bad I missed last year when they . . . *Uh-oh.*

I skidded to a stop and yelled at my fellow tunnelers. "Hey, wait a minute. What did you mean by *lost*?"

Chapter 15

The Spy Cave Pony Castle

Splat. A shovel full of snow walloped me in the face just as I crawled into the entry tunnel with more supplies.

"Beamer, get out of the way," Secret Agent Snowmunk Bash apologized, shovel in hand.

I wiped chunks of snow off my glasses. "Well, maybe you'd like to get your own—"

"Hey, cool." Secret Agent Snowmunk Bonkers reached around Bash to snatch the beach buckets, gardening trowels and camping lantern I dropped when my world went white.

Jig Gobnotter slithered beneath Bonkers's arm and scamper-crawled around Bash. "Dibs on the red bucket."

With a snort, Jag dove around the other side of the Basher, twisting him into a heap atop Jig. She clamped her hands over both the red and yellow pails. "Ladies first."

"Hey!"

Jag snorted, shot down the tunnel into the hollowed-out snow cave and handed the red bucket to Mary Jane Morris. Mary Jane bowed. "Thank you, Jecolia Athalia Gobnotter. It's nice to see that some little kids have manners. Come along, Jecolia."

Is there some kind of rule that you have to act hoity-toity like Mary Jane when you turn thirteen? And why's she always slinging people's full names on them even when they're dusty ones that once belonged to great-great-grandparents who should have kept them?

Bash interrupted my brooding. "Are you going to sit there all day? We got a cave to dig out." He picked himself up off Jehoshaphat—I mean, Jig—and gazed after Mary Jane.

Jig popped up and grabbed the other trowel. "C'mon, Basher, let's go carve out more of the secret hideout."

Bash turned around with his shovel and followed Jig and Bonkers.

I shoved the snow that Bash threw in my face out the entrance. A snow cave. Snowmunks and their weirdo neighbors. And an Angel Without Knowing It in the chicken coop. *How soon before the snow melts so Mom and Dad can get through and I can get out of this North Pole nuttiness?* I brushed the rest of the snow outside and crawled down the five feet of tunnel through the snowdrift into the . . .

What an awesome snow cave!

An afternoon of all of us digging, scooping, dumping, scraping, molding, and shaping had built one huge igloo castle buried inside the biggest snowdrift I'd ever seen. Camping lights shone over walls and chairs and benches and shelves all made of snow.

Tyler rushed up and hugged my legs. "We build a big cave."

Lauren leaned against a snow wall near Mary Jane and Jag. "Is this how Ohioans live, Other Pig Boy?"

"Ask them. We never built snow caves in Virginia Beach. And c'mon, stop calling me that."

Bash paced our snowdrift fortress. "It's the best Secret Agent Snowmunk Secret Hideout ever."

I scraped a little more room into the ceiling a couple inches above. Mary Jane tapped my shoulder with a plastic beach shovel. "Don't break through the pony castle roof, Raymond William Boxby."

"It's not a castle. It's a secret hideout cave. Go fix your girly horsey wall."

"My pony castle wall's perfect. We're going to hang pictures on it, aren't we, Princess Jecolia and Princess Lauren?" Chocolate curls swirled as she spun on her boot heel.

Jag snorted—she always snorted—waved a garden trowel at me, and she and Mary Jane began carving pictures of ponies on the cave wall.

Lauren rolled teddy bear brown eyes at me, shrugged, picked up a bread knife from a snow table and joined the pony pictures carving.

Bonkers and Jig chunked more snow out of another wall to deepen the cave where the backyard sloped and snow drifted higher. They used the diggings to sculpt control panels onto the two snow chairs, with stools and side tables for secret agent weapons. Bash packed another layer of snow into the computer screen and control panel he fashioned so we could solve Secret Agent Snowmunk mysteries.

He tugged off his stocking cap and tossed it onto a snow table. "Told you snow caves are warm."

I inhaled crisp air that tasted, I don't know, clean, somehow. It smelled fresh.

Bonkers unzipped his coat. Something wriggled inside the hoodie he wore underneath. "It's Fred, my pet garter snake. I missed him. I'm trying to wake him by warming him up."

Jig ran over. "Let me see."

Bonkers reached down the neck of his hoodie and pulled out a coil of brownish-green scales with a white stripe down its back and yellow racing stripes down its sides. Tiny black beads of eyes shone from a diamond-shaped snake head. A forked, red tongue flickered from its mouth.

Bash grinned. "Sweet."

Lauren slid next to Bonkers and held out her hands. Bonkers poured nearly two feet of garter snake into her mittens. Lauren held Fred's brown and yellow face, his forked tongue flickering, up to her tanned nose. "He's cute. How long have you had him?"

"I rescued him last year. I think a bird hurt him. See the scar here where he was cut?"

"Yeah." Lauren kissed the top of the snake's head. "You do good work, Bonkers."

Bonkers beamed. Bash grinned. I tried to think of something to say. "So, how'd your dad die?" *Ugh. I didn't mean to say that.*

Lauren coiled the snake into the warmth of her mittens. "He got real sick. He didn't do anything to get sick. He just got sick really bad." She lowered her eyes. "It was horrible."

"He should have prayed. That's what I did last time I got sick." *Somebody make me shut up.*

Grizzly bear eyes tore into me. "He did, Other Pig Boy. Two weeks before he died, he said he loved Jesus. He wanted us to love Jesus too. But he died, anyway."

Lauren stuffed the snake inside her sweatshirt—my sweatshirt, the one Grandma gave me for Christmas—and thwacked my nose. She spun on a hand-me-down boot and headed for the girls. "Let's carve pony pictures into the walls."

I rubbed my nose and wondered what to do. I stepped toward the girls. Bonkers tugged at my sleeve. "Not now, Beams. Why don't you make a sandwich?"

I watched the girls a moment longer. None of them looked back. *I'm such a major jerk.*

I pulled jars of peanut butter and Aunt Tillie's homemade strawberry jam from my pockets and set them on the snow table next to the bread and hat cookies Bash brought from an earlier trip to the house for supplies. I pulled out a couple pieces of bread and plopped them with peanut butter.

"Ease up, Raymond William Boxby."

I nearly dropped the butter knife. I hadn't heard Mary Jane crunch up behind me. "Too much peanut butter?"

Mary Jane plucked the knife from my hand, balanced it on the edge of the cookie plate, and screwed the lid onto the jam jar. "No, I think you try too hard. Lauren talks. You listen."

I bit into my sandwich. Yep, too much peanut butter. "Sho I . . . *mmmgump* . . . should shut up sho I don't shay anything . . . *mmmp* . . . shtupid?"

"Don't help. Don't talk. Listen." She leaned closer and dropped her voice. "Now I need your help, and you're going to talk to me. I left groceries on Dick and Marge Johnson's porch this morning. Mrs. Johnson called the store later. Her bread and a jar of grape jelly were missing."

I gulped down peanut butter. "Did you pack them?"

Mary Jane stopped whispering. "Of course I did. I bagged her order myself. But listen to this. She said there were five loose eggs in the bag. I didn't put those there."

"So five eggs fell out of a carton. If they didn't break what's the problem?" I took another bite.

"She didn't order eggs, and I didn't pack any. But they were there."

I swallowed. "Anybody's chickens could have wandered off, hopped in a stray grocery sack, and laid eggs."

"One of the eggs was white, one tan"—Mary Jane leaned in again, and whispered—"and one blue. Your cousin practically signed his name to this caper."

"Wait, what?"

"Only one farm around here has a chicken that lays blue eggs." She waited for me to say something. I didn't. "Sebastian Nicholas Hinglehobb is playing tricks again, isn't he? He hid my gloves. He switched the bread and jelly for eggs. You might as well talk."

I gulped at the sandwich. *"Mmmrrrp."* I thought furiously while I chewed. "*Gulmp*. He thinks you're punking him."

Mary Jane sniffed. "I do not *punk* people." She rubbed her chin. "But for Sebastian, I might make an exception. He's always pulling stunts on me."

"I'm going to go hollow out another room. The snow cave needs a library. Bye."

I scooted away, but not before she fired off a last warning: "Don't play ignorant, Raymond William Boxby."

Bash cut me off before I made it to the far snow cave wall. "What color are her gloves?" he whispered.

"Who?"

"Mary Jane. What color are her gloves?"

"Pink. You know that."

"I mean, were there any colors besides pink?"

I glanced at Mary Jane, now back inside the cluster of pony sculptors. "I dunno. None of us are wearing our gloves inside the cave."

Bash held up his own bare hands. "Oh. Yeah. Well, watch her. The trap is set."

Bash smacked himself on the forehead and let out a yell. "Hey, Secret Agent Snowmunks, we forgot to build the mast-odon traps."

Chapter 16

Mastodons, Snakes, and Snowmunks

I nearly choked on my peanut butter. Bonkers scooted into a control panel chair and fiddled with snow buttons he'd built onto the armrests. "Excellent. Mastodon traps." He patted another button into place. "Why do we need mastodon traps?"

Bash paced the snow floor. "We're Secret Agent Snowmunks, right? So the International Mastodon Spies will want to find our secret hideout, right?"

Jig jumped onto a snow footstool and pumped his fist. "We can't let 'em, can we? No mastodons." He swatted at the red hair poking from beneath the bill of a baseball cap with earflaps. "What's a mastodon?"

Mary Jane rolled her eyes. "Mastodons were hairy elephants with curly tusks. They died centuries ago. They're extinct."

Secret Agent Snowmunk Bash paced, chewing on his tongue. "Yep, they stink, all right. Dirty, rotten scoundrels. They'd just love to thunder through a Secret Agent Snowmunk hideout. We gotta build a mastodon trap."

Princess Jag snorted. Queen Mary Jane stamped her boot. "There are no such things as mastodons."

Bash shook his head. "That's what they want you to think. They're international spies. They hide in trees."

A peanut butter haze clogged my words. "They were the size of elephants. They can't hide in trees. Stop teasing the little kids."

Tyler tugged on Bash's sleeve. "'Cause they're 'bisible?"

Secret Agent Snowmunk Bonkers jumped out of his control panel chair. "Tyler's right. They're invisible. That's why nobody's seen any for years."

I groaned. "Bonk, don't encourage him."

Tyler ran around the snow chair. "'Bisible. 'Bisible. Mast dons 'bisible."

Bash slowly nodded his head. "Remember, Beamer, how Ma said it looked like a herd of elephants stampeded through my room? Invisible International Mastodon Spies."

I tossed the rest of my sandwich on the snow table. "Basher, maybe you better put your stocking cap back on. I think the cold froze your last brain cell."

"No time. We gotta build a mastodon trap." He grabbed his hat off the weapons table, yanked it over his head, and dove down the tunnel. Secret Agent Snowmunks Jig, Bonkers, and Tyler scampered after him.

A giggle leaked out of Lauren as Tyler whooped and cheered. "It's sweet when big boys aren't afraid to act silly with little kids."

I plopped down into one of the control panel chairs. "He's not acting," I muttered.

The Secret Agent Snowmunks returned, covered in snow and carrying icicles. Jig shook himself like a red-haired, freckled Chihuahua. "Wow, the snow's blowing again. We better head home, Sis."

Jag snorted at Jig and curtsied before Queen Mary Jane. "By your leave, m'lady."

Mary Jane inclined her head. "I shall walk with you. Your farm's across the road from our store. I suggest Christopher Joseph Dennison, Lauren Michelle Rodriguez, and Tyler Lewis Rodriguez, that you get home, too, if another blizzard's brewing."

Bonkers dumped his load of icicles on the floor and backed down the tunnel. "We'll get those Bad Guy Spy Mastodons tomorrow, Secret Agent Snowmunk Tyler. C'mon, Dad just pulled in on his snowmobile to drive us home."

Tyler tossed aside the two icicles he carried and chased after Bonkers. "Ride, ride, we're gonna ride the 'nomobile again." Lauren slipped out after them. Mary Jane, Jig, and Jag followed.

I headed for the tunnel. Bash pulled me back. "Not yet. We gotta set the trap."

"Tyler's gone. You can stop acting like a little kid."

"Who's acting? This'll be fun."

I listened to the growing growl of the wind and the fading roar of Mr. Dennison's snowmobile. "Another blizzard's coming. We've got to get home."

"We *are* home, Ray-Ray Sunbeam Beamer. We live here. Well, I do."

"If it keeps snowing like this, I'll never get home and then I'll live here too. And stop calling me that."

Bash smushed one icicle, pointy end up, in the middle of the hideout floor. "Plant these all over. If a big, ol' mastodon lumbers into our hideout, he'll prick his big ol' toe and run away."

I planted an icicle. "I told you, the little kids are gone. You don't have to pretend about mastodons anymore."

Bash nudged me with his elbow and slapped another icicle in my hand. "C'mon, grow some joy."

Okay, so not *all* the little kids left the snow cave. "Don't you ever know when a game's over?" I shoved another skinny icicle into the floor, moved back a foot and jammed the next one in. It took a while to build our trap of tiny, crunchy, crinkly icicles. A patch of what looked like a giant hairbrush made up of shiny bristles with lots of broken pieces poked through the middle of the Secret Agent Snowmunk Cave.

Bash paced around it. "Cool."

I plopped into one of the control panel snow chairs. "Listen to that wind howling outside the tunnel. Maybe we ought to stay in here for a while."

Bash slid into the other control panel snow chair and fiddled with the buttons and toggles Bonkers built onto the armrests. "Told ya it was warm inside a snow cave. We're safe and—"

"Shh."

"What?"

"Did you hear that?"

"Hear what? The blizzard?"

I strained my ears. "There it is again. Above the roar of the storm. It sounds like a screech. It sounded a little bit like—your name."

Bash scooted back into the snow chair. "The mastodon spies. We need a periscope. Then we could spy on the spies."

"There are no such things as—"

Whomp. A large, hairy paw poked through the ceiling. I gasped. "It's a *mastodon*."

Another screech. Somehow, I figured mastodons would trumpet, like elephants at the zoo, but this one screeched. And it definitely sounded like Bash's name. No. *My* name. It was after *me*.

Crunch. More of the ceiling gave way as a second hairy paw smashed through the ceiling. More shrieking.

"Bash, we better scram."

He was already diving through the tunnel. I scrambled overtop him, gouging the tunnel ceiling. "Move it, slowpoke!"

"Stop it! You're collapsing the tunnel."

"It's not the tunnel. The whole cave is shuddering."

Whump. The snow cave caved in. The screeching—howling, now—nearly drowned out the blizzard. We didn't stick around.

"*Run!* The mastodon's after us!"

Bash lay on the floor of his bedroom, tossing the basketball toward the ceiling. I sat on the guest bed, back to the wall, throwing a supply of balled-up socks at the basketball, trying to knock it out of the air.

Grounded again. Evening chores were done, and we were stuck in Bash's room for the rest of the night.

"I still say you should have remembered your mom's boots are covered in fake rabbit fur."

Ball up. Toss sock. Miss.

"Ma hardly ever wears those boots. She thinks they look funny. Now they have peanut butter and strawberry jam all over 'em too. Besides, you're the one who yelled 'mastodon.'"

Ball up. Toss sock. Miss again.

"You're the one who kept talking about them. And you were going to leave me in the snow cave with the International Mastodon Spy."

Ball. Toss. Miss. Harder than it looks.

"How was I supposed to know it was Ma?"

"Yeah, if you'd recognized your own mom's boots, you'd have run faster."

Ball. Pillow this time. Still miss.

"Good thing Aunt Tillie put on that heavy coat before walking across the big yard to hunt for us in the blizzard. Crashing into our trap could have hurt."

"Ma said she didn't mean to. But she said she means to do something else now. About us."

Ball. My second pair of pants, empty legs flapping. Miss.

I shuddered. "She almost killed poor Fred."

"You woulda thought Ma'd never seen a snake before. But I've showed her lots of 'em."

I looked around for something else to throw. "I wonder when Fred slithered away from Lauren."

Bash rolled the basketball in his hands. "She noticed he was gone when she tried to give Fred back to Bonkers at the trailer. Bonkers called here."

"Oh, that was what that phone call was about."

"Yep. I told Bonkers that Fred was safe, but his nerves were shot from all that screaming." Bash flipped the ball a couple times. "Don't tell Ma that Fred's recovering in my sock drawer. Fred can't take any more screaming. We'll get him back to Bonk tomorrow."

Bash tossed the basketball at the ceiling. I threw a shoe. I missed. The shoe clattered off the wall. "So, genius, what fruit of the Spirit did we collect today by building a mastodon trap that only caught your mom in fuzzy boots?"

"Perseverance."

"Huh?"

"It's like patience."

"I know what perseverance is. How do you figure we got it?"

Ball. I whipped the quilt. No way—missed *again*.

"Hollowing out that cave inside the snow bank was hard work. We didn't quit. We persevered."

"Maybe."

"And the mastodon trap. We built it even though the blizzard chased away the other kids. Then we sat patiently waiting for a mastodon. And we would have gotten one, too, if Ma hadn't ruined the trap. See, we farmed the fruit of perseverance."

Ball. The other shoe. *Boing.* Hit! The ball and shoe clomped onto Bash's bed across from me. I dropped onto my belly and peered down at the Basher lying on the floor and shook my head. "You really are a few snowballs short of a fort."

Guess I just blew the fruit of kindness.

"Now let's see what happens with the other trap."

"Other trap?"

"The earmuffs were gone. Mary Jane had just enough time to snatch them from the chicken coop before leaving this afternoon."

"Jig and Jag were with her."

"Maybe she ducked them in the storm. Anyway, we'll know." Bash sat up. "I have a great idea for goodness."

"I'm afraid to ask."

"We're going to have a snow cow contest."

"A what?"

"It's like a snowman contest except we'll see who can build the goodest farm animal out of snow. And we'll find out who sprung the trap. How's that for goodness?"

"Goodest isn't a word. And we're grounded."

"We'll have all the kids over. And we'll bring the animals. Gulliver. Lulabelle. Mrs. Beakbokbok. They can be the judges. It'll be great!"

A pig? A cow? A chicken? Loose in the field of snow with Bash and the gang? And an earmuff trap? What's an earmuff trap? Oh yeah, it'll be great. Just great.

Chapter 17

Monkeys for Uncles

Grand Sculptor Bash paced before the line of snow cow contestants in a hay field at least three feet deep in snow. We couldn't sink all the way to the ground in the stuff, and we couldn't stay grounded inside the warm house to avoid it either. Aunt Tillie thought it a great goodness to let the Rodriguez kids build their first snowmen, so she suspended our sentence, even when I begged her not to. So there I stood in the line of snow cow contestants. The other kids dropped backpacks into the snow. I wondered what was in them. A bulging backpack sat half-sunk behind Bash too. Once again, my cousin forgot to tell me all the plans.

Bash stopped pacing. "Listen up, artists. Here are the snow cow rules."

Mary Jane planted a glove on her hip and rolled her eyes. "What do you know about rules, Sebastian Nicholas Hinglehobb?"

Lauren tugged on Jag's sleeve. "The rest of you call him Bash. How come you have nicknames like Bash, Beamer, Bonkers, Jig, and Jag? What's wrong with your real names?"

Jag, of course, snorted. "Jecolia Athalia Gobnotter, remember?"

Lauren crossed her arms. "Jecolia Athalia's a pretty name. It's not plain like Lauren. Bet it's not mistaken for a boy's name, either. People call me Tyler and my little brother Loren. I hate it." She stomped her boot.

Whump. A snowball splattered off Jag's shoulder. Snowball dust washed over Lauren's face. They both spun toward Bash, who clapped snow chunks off his gloves. "We're trying to have a snow cow contest. Listen up."

Jag's snorting nostril twitched. Mary Jane brushed snow off the tip of Lauren's nose. "That's why the kids call him Bash. We all want to bash him with snowballs."

Lauren giggled. Bash crinkled his eyebrows. "You're asking for it, Florida girl."

The three girls looked at each other. Tall Mary Jane puffed in a pink snowsuit. Skinny Jag, play dress poking from beneath her green coat, fluttering over green snow pants. Brown-eyed Lauren, with the color-splashed sweatshirt Grandma gave me jutting from beneath the winter coat Mary Jane wore last year. Their cheeks puffed and quivered as if moths fluttered inside their mouths.

They exploded into the most annoying girl giggles ever.

Bash stomped to the boys' end of the line. "Girls are impossible."

Bonkers snickered. "Herding your barn cats would be easier. They'd yowl less too."

Pow. Mary Jane plunked Bonkers in the chest with a snowball. *Whap. Whump.* Jag and Lauren winged snowballs at Bash. He fell backward over his backpack full of whatever was in there, rolled and came up flinging snow from each hand. "Take that. And that."

Giggling girls ducked as Bash laughed and charged before tripping in the snow and landing face first at Mary Jane's boots.

Tyler scooped up two tiny handfuls of white stuff and heaved it heavenward in a glittery spray. "Throw snow. Throw snow!"

It was on. Bonk, Jig, and I zipped around, dodging incoming while hurling outgoing. *Splat.* Stinging cold melted quickly. Shivers of snow juice trickled down our necks and inside coats and snowsuits. Must have evaporated quickly because I didn't notice it for long.

Whap. For the next half hour, we plunged across the field, pelting each other with snowballs, tackling anyone we could catch, high-diving into drifts, making snow angels, and heaving piles more of snowballs.

Splot. Somehow we all ended up lying in the snow, cooling off in one, big giggling clump, all chattering at once.

"Awesome."

"Way cool."

"I got you good."

"Yeah, until I made you eat snow."

Tyler loosened himself from the mess and crawled over legs and arms and boots until he collapsed on top of Bash.

The little boy wrapped his arms around my cousin. "Thank you, Unca Bash-Bash. You're fun."

The glow from Bash's face nearly melted the snow. "Uncle? D'ja hear that, Beams? He called me uncle."

I swatted a splash of snow at Bash. "Well, I'll be a monkey's uncle."

"Nope. That's my dad. An uncle to a monkey."

"Hey!"

We lined up again, a disheveled bunch of kids in a disheveled hay field full of snow. Bash paced in front of the troops. "Now, let's have our snow cow contest."

"I'm in."

"Why not?"

"Cool."

Snort.

Lauren raised her hand. "*Uncle* Pig Boy, what's a snow cow?"

A quick grin flashed across Grand Sculptor Bash's face. "It's like a snowman contest. Only we build animals—cows, chickens, pigs, horses, sheep, goats, stuff like that."

"Oh. How do we know who wins?"

"The judges will choose."

Jag snorted, red ponytails spilling from beneath her stocking cap. "I suppose you'll be the judge."

Bash shook his head. "Nope. We'll bring out the experts. A cow. That's why it's a snow cow contest. I'll ride Lulabelle Liechtenstein Daffodil Lee over here from the cow barn and she'll choose the best."

"Bash, your mom and dad told us . . ."

"Never to ride cows on the road again. We're not. We're riding them to the hay field to judge the contest. And probably Gulliver J. McFrederick the Third. It can be a snow pig contest too."

Bonkers raised Tyler's hand. "We call the pig."

Tyler squealed. "We ride the pig. We ride the pig. Unca Beamer, wanna ride the pig with us?"

Uncle Beamer? I cringed. I'm nobody's uncle. Uncles have to babysit and change diapers and junk. I crossed my arms. "I don't ride pigs. I don't change diapers, either, so don't ask."

Lauren marched up and thwacked my nose. "Don't you tease my little brother, Other Pig Boy. He doesn't wear diapers. Do you?"

I stepped back and covered my nose. "No, I don't wear diapers. But he's a baby."

"I'm not a baby. I'm this many." Tyler held up a mittened hand that didn't show any fingers.

Lauren leaned in, her nose-thwacking hand wound up and ready for take-off. "He's four. He doesn't wear diapers. You apologize right now."

I back-pedaled so fast that I slipped and thumped onto the seat of my pants. Lauren glared down at me with those grizzly bear eyes. Behind her, Mary Jane smirked. "What's the matter, Raymond William Boxby? Are you chicken?"

I scooted back. "I can't ride the pig because I'm . . . I'm getting a chicken. Yeah. I'm building a snow chicken, and I'm bringing Mrs. Finley Q. Ruffed-something-feather Beakbokbok as a judge. That's why."

"See that you do." Lauren spun and stomped away.

Mary Jane grabbed my arm and pulled me up. "She told you."

"Yeah, I guess. Thanks."

I started to pull my arm away, but Mary Jane held on. "Raymond."

"Yeah."

Mary Jane leaned in to whisper into my wool-capped ear. "I delivered oatmeal and laundry soap to the Pifers this morning. Mrs. Pifer lost her wool scarf, the one silhouetted with deer. She hangs it on the pegs with their barn coats and hats. It disappeared."

I closed my eyes. "And?"

"Mrs. Pifer showed me what she found instead. Red ink on the door knob. Red ink on the peg. And on the windowsill—"

"Red ink?"

"Yes. And two eggs—one white and one green. Green, Raymond."

"You're saying that two chickens waddled into the Pifers's breezeway, spilled red ink, laid white and green eggs, and waddled away in a scarf? How do two chickens share a scarf?" When I try to think under pressure, dumb things blurt out of my mouth on their own.

Mary Jane froze me with laser blue eyes. "Chickens don't waddle." She waddled, or possibly strutted, until her nose practically touched mine. "What I want to know from you, Raymond William Boxby, is if your cousin is up to some of his pranks."

I shook my head, probably too hard. "No, honest. Bash hasn't left my sight that long. I keep hoping he will so I can sneak back to bed and read comic books. But he hasn't.

Sticks to me all the time. No way. It wasn't us. Him, I mean. It wasn't him. Or me either."

The more I protested, the more pathetic I sounded. Mary Jane folded her arms. "You'd tell me if he did."

No. "Sure thing, Mary Jane."

She stared. I gulped. She put a glove to her chin and weighed my answer. I dropped my eyes to her boots. "It wasn't us."

Mary Jane dropped her arm. "Okay. But something freakish is going on, and that usually means Sebastian's involved. You watch him for me."

"Yeah, fine. Will do." *Maybe.*

Mary Jane trotted toward Lauren. I slumped and staggered toward my assigned snow sculpting zone. Time to get started.

Bash zipped in front of me. "What color are her gloves?"

"Who's?"

Bash looked left, right, then stepped closer and whispered. It was a great day for whispering. "Mary Jane. What color are her gloves?"

"Pink. You know that."

"I mean besides pink. Was there anything on them?"

"There was some gunk in the palm of one of the gloves. She probably spilled some groceries. Cranberries, maybe."

Bash pumped his fist. "I knew it. She's leaving her fingerprints all over this caper. We've got her red-handed."

"What—"

"I'll tell you later. Keep an eye on her, Super Spy Beamer." He barreled back to his pile of snow.

I tugged the glasses off my face and looked around. Blurry kids rolled blurry snowballs and stacked them onto blurry snow mounds. I slid my glasses back into place. The kids and snow popped back into focus. But what was happening around here—blurry. Nothing but hazy, fuzzy, smudgy, blotchy blurs. *Someone please tell me what's going on.*

Chapter 18

Snow Cows, Ducks, and Chickens

I hated building a snow chicken. The beak fell off a lot.

Bonkers eyed my chicken as he pushed past, rolling another big ball toward a snow pig big enough to munch on a house. “Nice duck.”

“It’s not a duck, it’s a chicken. Stop waddling away with all my snow.”

Bonkers patted his Goliath pig snowball. “You already have all the snow you need for a duck that little.”

“It’s a chicken.”

Bonk gouged a hunk out of the chicken's back. "Chicken backs are flatter, even slouched, like this. They could wear tiny saddles."

"Um, thanks, doctor."

Bonkers saluted. "Not yet. I'll send you a bill after veterinary school in twenty years." He leaned into his snowball, rolling up ribbons of the white stuff like a big ol' ball of Silly String.

Tyler waded over, dropped a dress he dragged, and smoothed the scoop back. "S'okay, Unca Beamer. I like duckie."

"It's a chick . . . Ah, nuts, it's a duck." I repacked snow into the sloped bird back. "And stop calling me tha . . ."

Tyler had been hunched over, tiny hands flittering through the snow. Now he stood, eyes as big and warm as my calf Amy's, a little snowman couched in his cupped hands. "For you, Unca Beamer."

A butterfly flickered from my stomach into my throat. It got stuck. It was more like moth size. I gulped it down. "Thanks." I carefully took the snowman from Tyler's mittens and set it on the snow duck chicken's back. "Ta-dah, it's the Duck King."

"You funny, Unca Beamer."

"You're a good snowman builder—Nephew Tyler."

The little guy giggled. "You make good duckies." He reached for the collar of the dropped dress and pushed off through the snow.

"Um, Tyler, why are you dragging a dress?"

"It's for Unca Bash."

I followed Tyler and the dragged dress to the snow cow, which looked more like an army tank with horns. Tyler ran the last few steps, flinging the dress. "Here, Unca Bash."

"Thanks, Ty. Uh-oh, I think our snow cow needs to lose a few pounds to fit into this dress." Bash karate-chopped a couple chunks from the middle of the army tank with horns. Tyler kicked at either a fat leg or tank tread.

I scooped up the blue-flowered dress. "Basher, isn't this your mom's Sunday dress?"

Bash puttered with either a cow nose or tank gun. "Nope. She hangs up her good stuff. This was at the bottom of a basket of old, wrinkled junk."

"The laundry basket?"

"Why would she wash her good dresses? She only wears them on Sundays. I get ten or twelve days out of the same jeans."

"Yeah, we know." My head hurt. "Okay, so *why* would you, a boy, take the best Sunday dress from your mom, a girl?"

Bash added three inches of snow onto the horns—or possibly the periscope. "Gear for the snow cow, of course. We all brought stuff. Didn't I tell you?"

"No."

"Oh yeah. You were busy beating your head against the wall. I've got more stuff in my backpack you can use."

I wiped snowflakes off my glasses for a better look at the competition. In her section of the field, Mary Jane fitted a pink sun hat onto a skinny snow goat that already wore a yellow neck scarf and red, high-heeled shoes.

Across the way, Jag and Lauren poked Oreo cookie eyes into a snow pony. I wondered how they got the one to wink. Jag wiped crumbs off her lips. Oh.

On his section of the contest field, Bonkers twisted ugly orange carrot fangs into his giant snow pig. "Wild boars have tusks."

"Um, do wild boars live in the woods over there?"

"Nope, but I keep hoping. That would be so cool. The boars against the bears."

I shot a quick look at the woods beyond the hay field, between Bash's farm and Bonkers's place. "I thought you guys told me no bears lived in those woods."

"Yeah, I keep hoping about that too."

I hoped, too, but not the same hope.

On the other side of my snow duck chicken, Jig struggled to push a head atop a regular old snowman. I ran over to help. "I thought we were supposed to be building farm animals."

I centered the head. Jig smashed snow between it and the shoulders, sort of like snow glue. "I'm building the farmer." He pulled a patched pair of overalls and work gloves from his own backpack. "Dad gave me some of his old farm clothes. The hat's one of my own."

He handed me a red International Harvester baseball cap. "Reach that on his head for me. Thanks."

After we draped the duds over the snow farmer, I poked through Bash's crammed backpack to see what I might find for my snow duck chicken. "Basher, you've got chocolate syrup in here."

"Oh, yeah, thanks. Throw it here. It's to make the brown spots on the snow cow."

"So what's the strawberry jam for?"

Mary Jane waved. "Over here. The snow pony is having tea and jam."

Lauren set a snow saucer stacked with snow biscuits in front of the pony. While Mary Jane plopped jam onto snow biscuits on a snow saucer, I tried to apologize to Lauren. "Look, I'm sorry about calling Tyler a baby."

Lauren packed snow into the shape of a teacup. "Fine."

"I don't mean to say stupid things."

"Then don't, Other Pig Boy." She positioned the teacup next to the saucer.

"It's just that I never talked to a kid whose dad died."

Grizzly bear eyes growled. "Is it fun for you? I'm having a blast." Lauren rocketed to her feet and lurched to the other side of the pony.

"Wait. No. What I meant—"

Mary Jane shoved the empty jam jar into my hands and shot me a warning look. Jag threw an arm around Lauren and snorted. "Stop making her cry, you meanie."

"But I don't . . ." My stomach wobbled. "It's just that I'm trying to figure out how . . ."

Lauren's chin quivered against Grandma's sweatshirt. I barely heard her. "I know."

I rolled the empty jam jar between my hands. Lauren gurgled. Jag glared and wiped a tear from Lauren's cheek. Mary Jane, her arm now around Lauren's other shoulder, shook her head and waved me away.

"Yeah, well . . . thanks for the talk." And with another stupid thing said, I tromped back to the backpack, dropped the empty jam jar into the backpack, found a box of yellow goldfish crackers, and dumped them all over the snow duck chicken.

Oh great. Somebody smudged red ink all over the cracker box. So Bash caught me in his trap, too, whatever it is? What else could go wrong?

"Beams! It's time for the judges. Go get Mrs. Finley Q. Ruffeather Beakbokbok from the chicken coop."

Oh. Yeah.

Chapter 19

Flight of the Snow Cow Judges

I met Bash and Bonkers on the way back to the hay field.

"Bash, in the chicken coop, there's a—"

"Not now, Beamer." Cowback King Bash sat atop the broad, swaying back of Lulabelle Liechtenstein Daffodil Lee. He put a gloved finger to his lip. "The trap."

"But—"

Bash shook his head. He steered the giant, shaggy, black-and-white cow by the horns as she plowed her bulk through several feet of snow.

Bonkers trotted behind, leading the rust-red hog Gulliver J. McFrederick the Third. Tyler rode piggyback and clapped. *"Lookit me, Unca Beamer, lookit me."*

I followed, a white hen cradled in one arm.

The judges were on their way to the art show.

"Ow." The crazy chicken pecked my thumb again. Bash snickered. "Ray-Ray Sunbeam Beamer's getting pummeled by a six-pound chicken."

"Shut up and tell her to stop pecking me."

"You're the one who grabbed Lizzie Longhorn Leghorn. Where's Mrs. Finley Q. Ruffeather Beakbokbok? She's nicer."

"Not to me, she isn't." I tucked Lizzie under my other arm and buried my hands in my pockets. Lizzie took a swipe at my chin. "Bash, something wacko's going on in the chicken coop."

"Not now, Beams. It's time to start the judging." Bash slid off Lulabelle's back, plunging into the deep snow in the center of the snow cow contest hay field and plucked Lizzie from my arms. Old Dragonbreath turned into Chicken Tender, practically cooing in Bash's arms.

"Okay, kids, the judges are here. May the best farm animal win."

He set Lizzie atop the snow, where she puffed up her feathers and shook like a hissing cat before running at me to peck my boots. "Cut it *out*."

Bonkers aimed Gulliver at the wild snow boar and dismounted. Gulliver sniffed the snow pig, the flat disc of his nose bobbing. He ate a carrot tusk.

Lulabelle wandered toward the snow cow. With her long, slobbery cow tongue, Lulabelle licked a big hunk of chocolate spot like it was a snow cow cone. Bash tried to push her away. "You'll ruin it."

Lauren ducked behind the snow pony. "Cows are huge close up. Is she safe?"

Jag snorted. "Not if Bash trained her."

Tyler took a run at Lulabelle, pushing on her barrel belly with little, mittened hands. "Go 'way, cow. Eat the pony."

A shrill scream shattered the not-so-silence. "Get away from my tea and jam!"

Gulliver rooted through the fancy feasting at the snow pony's tea party. Glops of strawberry jam covered his snout, mixing with the yellow flakes of Goldfish crackers no longer on my snow duck chicken.

Mary Jane swished her arms. "Shoo, pig. Shoo, pig." Instead, Gulliver sat on the snow goat and grinned his piggy grin.

Lulabelle munched an Oreo cookie eye off the snow pony. Lizzie the hen flapped up to the snow farmer and came down wearing the red International Harvester hat.

Jig scrambled after the hen. "Come back with my cap."

Lizzie stutter-ran full feathers ahead and pecked Gulliver's rust-colored hamstrings. The hog bolted upright and ran. *"Rweeeeet. Rweeeeet."* One front foot sliced right through the snow goat's sun hat. The ripped hat shot up Gulliver's leg and whapped his pork barrel chest like loose straw armor.

Mary Jane moaned. "That pig poked a hole in my bonnet."

Gulliver ran until he crashed into Lulabelle, who crunched the other cookie eye. The white hen, now draped with the yellow scarf to go with the red cap dangling from her neck, gave chase. *"Bwak, bwak, bwaaaak."*

Gulliver tried to run right up Lulabelle's back.

"Mmmwaaaaa." Lulabelle bolted. It's one thing to allow a wispy farm kid on your back, but serving as a launching pad

for a 300-pound chicken hog afraid of a chicken is another matter.

Tyler clapped. "Yay, Unca Bash. Funny."

Bash zoomed past trying to catch the cow. *"Beamer, grab that chicken."*

"Tell Bonkers. He wants to be a veterinarian."

Bonkers dived out of the way. "I don't make house calls for leghorns as mad as snow hens."

"Mmmwaaaa." Lulabelle bounded into the snow cow, tangling up in Aunt Tillie's Sunday dress.

A couple more leaps, jumps, and bounds, and a few shakes, and somehow she wore the dress. Her massive cow head poked out of the unbuttoned neck of the dress. The skirt end flowed and flapped from her withers to her brisket.

"Mmmwaaa." The cow took off at full gallop across the field and toward the house, Aunt Tillie's Sunday dress billowing like a blue-flowered flag.

Gulliver seemed to think the plan a good one and charged after her, straw hat flapping. Behind them ran a squawking hen, a red cap bouncing on its back, a long, yellow scarf fluttering behind.

Mary Jane, Jag, and Lauren chased after them. *"Come back here with my scarf and hat."*

Bonkers drifted toward the woods. "I think I hear my dad calling me."

Bash plopped down in the snow. "We might as well wait for it."

"Good, because I need to tell you about the chicken coop. Mrs. Beakbokbok ran behind that stack of boards against the far wall. I couldn't reach her, but I found a folded-up sleeping bag. A pink, purple, and orange paisley sleeping bag."

Bash stared at the mad caravan streaking toward the house. "So?"

"It's got to be the one from the garage. But it's in the chicken coop."

He shrugged. "Pops must have moved it."

"To the chicken coop? Why? And we take care of the chickens, not your dad." I kicked at the snow. "By the way, what is *it* that we're waiting for?"

A shriek like a fire siren pierced the crisp winter air. *"Why's the cow wearing my dress? Se-baaaas-tiannnnnnnnnnn!"*

"That." Bash sighed.

Tyler jumped up and down. "Who won, Unca Bash?"

"I dunno, Ty, buddy. But I know who lost."

The animals and girls rounded the house for their second lap. Lizzie nestled in the scarf on the porch. Aunt Tillie took the hen's place in the chase, without even putting on her fuzzy boots.

Bash stood up. "C'mon, we better go catch the animals."

I took Tyler's hand and followed Bash's slow trot. "Yeah, then it's us who'll catch it. Tell me about the goodness part again, turkey brain."

"You worry too much."

"Somebody around here has to. There's a lot to worry about."

Like how do we fix Tyler and Lauren? Whose chickens are leaving eggs on back porches? How'd the ugly sleeping bag get from the garage to the chicken coop? Why was it folded now, instead of rolled up? Where'd the missing gloves come from, and where did they go? Why is bread disappearing from grocery bags? Had I remembered to pray today about any of this? Is it too late to start? Or should I just wait until the next stupid thing I say that makes Lauren cry? Why was I asking myself so many questions?

I hated this.

Chapter 20

How to Climb a Hay Fort with Your Teeth

Bash pulled shut the big, rolling door of the cow barn. "Maybe you imagined it."

I shivered. "Nobody could imagine a pink, purple, and orange paisley sleeping bag like that. I'm telling you, Bash, it was there yesterday afternoon."

"So how come you didn't show me last night?"

"Your mom's screeching kinda shook me up."

Bash packed a snowball and heaved it over the tractor

shed. "You'd think she'd never seen a cow wearing a Sunday dress before."

"Probably not. Especially not *her* Sunday dress." I rolled a snowball and threw. It splattered on the roof of the shed. "Anyway, I remembered this morning, but it's gone. Like the blue gloves and red muffs. And more eggs. And why's the chicken coop so clean when I hardly sweep it anymore? Does something have the hens rattled?"

Bash rolled three snowballs and juggled them. "What's Mary Jane up to?"

I rolled two snowballs to juggle. "She thinks it's you." I dropped one of my snowballs. "Is it?"

"'Course not. I'm not dragging that mugly ugly sleeping bag around." He peppered all three snowballs over the shed roof in mid-juggle. "So you wanna build something inside today?"

I slung my other snowball. I heard it smack the shed roof as I turned for the house. "But your mom said we're not allowed to use hammers and nails inside again."

"Not inside the house." Bash turned and sprinted down one of his snow trails. "The haymow."

I don't know why Uncle Rollie calls the upstairs of the hay barn a mow—pronounced like "ow." It's spelled m-o-w, like when you cut grass. That's what baling hay is—cutting field grass and packing it into bales. In the summer, Aunt Tillie puts up cans of green beans, sliced carrots, peaches and pears to eat in the winter. Baling hay is like canning for cows. And it's stored in the haymow, which is like a giant attic above the barn.

I slogged along the snow trail, up the ladder-stairs of the hay barn and through the trap door in the attic floor. Bash stared up at a wall of hay stacked in a hatched pattern like a solid brick warehouse twelve or thirteen feet tall.

"Can you see it, Ray-Ray Sunbeam Beamer?"

"Stop calling me that. I see thousands of blocky, scratchy, itchy bales of hay."

"Not hay bales. A fortress."

"What fortress?"

"With towers, tunnels, laser canons, secret passages, and a control room."

"What fortress?"

"No invader shall overcome the Castle Fortress of Count Bash the Conqueror of the Galaxy."

"What fortress?"

"The one we're going to build out of the hay bales."

"Oh. . . . Hey, wait. What?"

"Hay bales are like Lego blocks without the knobby things on top. You can use 'em to build castles, an' caves, an' mazes, an' anything you can build with Legos. But lots bigger."

I'll say. Uncle Rollie's hay bales measure about three feet long, a foot-and-a-half wide and more than a foot tall. And they're heavy.

Bash scaled the wall of hay. "C'mon, slow pokey puppy."

I dug my fingers into cracks and crevices between the blocks of hay and climbed. Sprinkles of hay dust fluttered down my nose. About seven rows high, I looked up—no way was I looking down—to see the bottoms of Bash's boot toes. Spitting hay droppings from my mouth, I tipped my head back another fraction of an inch. My crazy cousin held one of the heavy hay bales over the edge, and it looked like he was going to—

"Look out below!"

"Yeow." I let go and tried to fall faster than the grassy brick coming straight for my head.

Ker-splat. Swoosh-whoosh. I crashed to the wooden floor, curled and rolled.

Ka-thunck. The hay bale smashed to the floor, nipping my back. The exploding air shot hay dust all around me. I screamed, sneezed, and yelled all at once. *"Aaiiii-ahchoo-numbskull."*

"*Awesome* move, Beamer."

I sat up and shook crunchy weeds and hay dust out of my sleeves, collar, pockets, ears, and . . . *snort* . . . my nose. A dried, brown clover shot out of my mouth with the words I spat at the Basher: "You threw a hay bale at me."

"Did not. You trespassed in the landing zone. The climbing zone is over there."

"This is where you climbed."

Bash disappeared from the edge of the twelve-foot hay wall. "It wasn't a landing zone then. It was *my* climbing zone. Your climbing zone is on the other end of the Castle Fortress of Count Bash the Conqueror of the Galaxy."

I shook hay stalks from my wool hat. "How come you get to name the fortress?"

"I climbed it first. Everybody knows first one up gets to name the mountain."

"I thought it was a dumb fortress, not a stupid mountain."

Bash reappeared at the edge holding another hay bale. "Duh, the best super fortresses are built on mountain tops. Here's another hay bale."

I dove out of the way just before another big block thunked to the floor. "Stop throwing hay at me!"

"Sorry, Beams. I thought you moved out of the landing zone."

"Let me get up there and I'll show you a landing zone."

The Basher hooted. "C'mon, get up here and help build Castle Fortress of Count Bash the Conqueror of the Galaxy and Outpost of Duke Beamer the Hay-Brained."

"You're as funny as a geography pop quiz."

I brushed hay out of my hair and tossed the hat aside. It really was warmer in the hayloft. A calico barn cat purred itself into my lap. I peeled off my gloves and scratched its ears. No little kid cousin was going to show me up. I'm six months older, after all.

I set the calico cat on the floor and stood. I clutched clumps of hay above me, dug boot toes into the cracks between bales and started pulling myself up. It was like one of those climbing walls at the mall, only without toeholds. Or handholds. Or safety harness. Nothing to it.

The calico cat scampered past me, hopped over the top, and peered down, waiting. "Easy for you to say," I muttered.

Without peeking down, I wriggled up a sheer wall of all ten layers of stacked hay bales. I threw my left arm over the top bale, wrapped my fingers around the twine holding it together, and pulled.

The bale tipped. Yeow. Instead of pulling myself up, I pulled the top bale right off the top of the wall, like pulling a giant brick off the top of a castle parapet. The hay Lego blocks needed the knobby things to snap the bales in place.

I ducked and hung on as the bale flipped over my head and flew to the floor. I chomped into the bale closest to my nose. I flopped around in mid-air, hanging on only by my teeth. Arms and legs flailed. I bit harder. What if this bale fell too? I'd better learn to fly, and fast, that's what.

Chapter 21

Building a Hay Fort Where the Bats Live

I could either hang by my teeth to a wall of hay—which tastes like dried-out salad—or I could scramble.

I churned my legs like riding a bicycle. A knee hit a crack between blocks. I wedged it in good and planted the knee on the hay brick below it. I threw my arm over the bale I chewed and swung my other leg over the other end of the bale. I held my breath, waiting to see if the bale wobbled. It didn't.

I unclamped my jaw and rolled the rest of the way atop the bale. I sat nine rows up, in the spot where the toppled bale used to be, spitting hay. I pressed my back against the tenth row. My heart thudded, threatening to push me forward into space. I gathered my feet beneath me and pushed, propelling myself up and backward onto the top of the hay wall and as far away from the edge as possible.

I'd made it.

The calico cat nuzzled my cheek. Lying flat on my belly, I scooted toward the edge and peered over. Twelve or thirteen feet sure seems higher when you're up there looking down. A *lot* higher. I could get a nosebleed. This far up, those specks way down there on the hard, hard floor could be mice. Or rats. Or horses. We were way, way, waaaay—

Bash snatched me around the ankles and dragged me backward. "Ah, quit whimpering, Duke Beamer the 'Fraidy-Cat Chicken-Heart. We have a fortress to build."

My knees wobbled when I stood on the long, flat rooftop of thousands of bales crammed together like bricks without cement to hold them in place. Yes, I knew Uncle Rollie packed his bales solid in a hatched pattern that held them stable, but did the bales know that? "I'm not a 'fraidy-cat chicken. It's just—"

Blam. I smashed my forehead on a roof rafter.

Bash backhanded my shoulder. "Careful, Beamer. You don't want to wake the bats."

I spun around. "Bats? What bats?"

"The ones that hang on the rafters and eat the bugs, Duke Chicken-Cat."

I blinked hard at rows of rafters. Two empty bird nests. No birds. And no bats. "I don't see any bats."

"Nuts. They must have flown south for the winter."

"Bats don't fly south for . . . Actually, I don't care where they fly as long as it's not in my hair."

"They don't eat hair."

I clamped my hands over my head and ducked as I walked. "They might forget."

Bash ran across the hay-top to the center of the loft. "We'll start digging here."

"With what?"

"It's just an expression, Duke Chicken-Cat. I mean we're gonna start pulling bales out of the center. It'll be our dungeon. Or a lion pit. I haven't decided."

Bats. Birds. Lions. What next?

Fortress Builder Bash lugged a bale from the middle of the hay-top and huffed and puffed it over to the edge where we climbed. "C'mon, Duke, start digging."

I yanked up the next bale by the twin bands of baling twine holding it together. The bale bounced a bit as the twine bit into my bare palms. I staggered the bale over to the edge, almost tripping over another one of the barn cats, a fat orange one. "Watch it, kitty. You almost knocked me off the wall."

I turned just as Bash let go of the next one, letting it whomp into my shins. I hopped over it, ducking my head so I wouldn't hit the rafters. "Watch it, Count Bats in the Belfry. You almost knocked me off the wall."

"We're teaching you ballet. Stop being a 'fraidy cat—no wait, the cats aren't 'fraid—stop being a 'fraidy mouse and grab some more bales."

I looked around real fast, trying to see everything at once. "You have mice up here too?"

"Sure. That's what the lions, I mean, cats are for, Duke Chicken-Mousey."

"They don't scare me. I just don't like mice crawling up my pants."

Bash kicked my foot. “Can’t. Your pant legs are tucked into your boots.”

“Okay then.”

We dragged bales out of the top layer until we had an opening about six feet square. We leaned over and pulled up the next layer. Fortress Builder Bash unzipped his winter coat and hung it over a rafter. “Okay, Duke Chicken-Mousey, time to drop down the hole and pull up the next tier and chuck it out.”

“Stop calling me that.” I slung my winter coat over the rafter next to Bash’s. I wish I hadn’t left my hat below. You never know about bats.

We dug until the pit was about as deep as we were tall. That far down, we either stood bales on end and shoved them up and over the top of the pit, or we each grabbed an end of a bale, swung it for counts of “one, two,” and slung it out of the pit on “three.”

I dropped onto one of the last two bales of the layer and sucked wind. “Give me a moment.”

“’Sokay, Beamer. We’re leaving these two here. They’ll be the ones we stand on so we can peek over the top of our spy hole.”

“I thought you said it was a lions’ den or a dungeon.”

“Or a spy hole.” We climbed back onto the hay roof. Bash wiped an arm across his sweaty brow and peered back into the spy hole. “Ah ha! It’s a lion pit. See, three cats—I mean, lions—already are napping at the bottom.”

Three cats curled up in a ball against one of our stepping bales. “A lions’ den like the one in the Bible that the king threw Daniel in?”

“Yep.”

I scratched my head, but carefully—bats can be sneaky. "Your dad doesn't have any lions hidden around here, does he?"

"Nah. He said he'd get a bunch of baboons first to go with the one he already has, but we don't have any baboons, so I dunno what he meant. Now, c'mon, we gotta build the towers."

"What?" By the time I dragged myself across the hay fort roof, Bash was assembling the bales we pulled out of the lion's den into a series of three-sided towers along the edge of the hay wall. "Beamer, help me lift this bale in place."

I saw it now—a series of turrets. We stacked the hay so that the front of each turret contained a peephole big enough to fire a slingshot through. If anyone tried to attack, we'd be safe inside the turrets and able to rain down on them a steady stream of . . . of . . .

"Um, Bash, we don't have any weapons."

Bash grabbed the next bale. "We're gonna use our water blaster squirt guns."

I peeked through a hay turret window. "We don't have any attackers, either." I looked again. "Are we going to have any?"

Fortress Builder Bash pushed a wall of hay bales into place between the turrets. "I'm trying to figure out how to lure Mary Jane up here. Then we'll get her with our squirt guns."

"In the winter? Basher, she'll freeze."

Bash pulled a handkerchief from his back pocket and wiped a river of sweat off my forehead. "Are you freezing?"

"Well, no . . ."

"Okay then, Duke Chicken-Mousey, grab your coat and let's get the squirt guns."

Somebody was about to get soaked, and I hoped it wasn't us. Not again.

Chapter 22

Attack of the Whac-A-Moles

I stood on tiptoes and peeked over my turret. Nothing. "Is she coming?"

Bash set an orange water pistol on the ledge of the hay turret window. "Mary Jane said she would. I called as soon as we went inside. I didn't want to dig out the water guns and fill 'em unless she was coming."

I squinted at the trap door in the floor where Mary Jane would come up the ladder-stairs. Bash pointed his water gun. "As soon as her head pops through the trap door, soak her."

Except for the occasional gust of winter wind outside and the soft snicker-snores of the barn cats sleeping in the lions' den way behind us, the haymow remained quiet. No Mary Jane voice yelling hello. No Mary Jane footfalls tromping up the ladder-stairs. No Mary Jane gasps of surprise at seeing an awesome fort.

I sat behind my turret and squeezed off a test burst from my super water shooter. "Isn't this kind of mean?"

"Nah. The speedometer is thirty-five today."

"Thermometer."

"That means it's above freezing."

"It's still colder than a refrigerator."

"Ah, I'm not gonna really send her home like an ice cube." Bash nodded toward a bulging backpack stashed inside one of the hay turrets between us. "I brought Ma's spare coat. When we give it to Mary Jane, it'll be an act of kindness. And we'll have another fruit of the Spirit crossed off the list."

I scratched my head with the top of a blue water pistol. Cold water drops rolled down my forehead and dripped off my nose. "How's squirting Mary Jane silly count for kindness?"

"She gets bored cooped up at her family's store all day. I try to help."

"You're a real gobble geek, Basher."

We both looked toward the door in the floor. Nothing moved. I thought about reaching up to the rafters for my coat, but Bash still was in his T-shirt so he'd be free to move quickly. If he could, I could.

I glanced behind us. "The cats sleeping in the lions' den sure sound funny."

"Lion snores can be like that."

I pulled a strand of hay from the turret and chewed on it. "Bash, I forgot why the king threw Daniel into the lions' den."

Bash chewed on his own piece of hay. "It's one of the best stories in the Farmin' and Fishin' Book. See, a bunch of guys who were jealous of Daniel tricked the king into making a law that for a month nobody could pray to anybody but the king. The king thought this was cool."

I spit out my hay. "Yeah, I remember now. It was a trap because the bad guys knew Daniel would do the right thing no matter what. So they got him thrown into a pit of hungry lions for praying to God."

Bash paced behind his turret. "Yep. But because Daniel obeyed God, God shut the mouths of the lions. And the next morning the king yelled down into the pit, 'Daniel, did your God rescue you from the lions?'"

I jumped up. "And Daniel yelled back, 'Yes.' And the king fed the bad guys to the lions instead."

"Yeah, it was way cool." Bash sat back down behind his turret and stared through the opening at the trap door.

"Awesome." I knelt back behind my turret and looked at the floor door. It was kind of like waiting for a lion to come up out of the den. No lion jumped up. I heard nothing but the snicker-snores of cats in the lions' den behind—

Fwap.

A snowball soaked the back of my neck. Snowball juices rolled down my back. I jumped in a frenzied, frozen-spine dance. "Not funny, Bash."

The Basher looked wild-eyed at me. *Fwap.* A juicy snowball splattered against his flyaway straw hair. "Yeow!"

Splot. Fwap. Whump. Splonk. A flurry of snowballs pounded into us as we tried to swat them away from behind our defenses. I jumped around, knocking three hay bales and a water gun to the floor far below. I stepped into a hole at the corners where four bales came together. My leg sank up past my knee and was trapped.

Splat. Whap. The snowball flurry continued. The Basher was stuck in his own hay hole. *Fwoomp. Splosh.*

Between the zings and whiz sounds of hurled snowballs, we heard a horrible sound—the snicker-snore of sleeping cats had turned into giggling.

Girls.

From the center of the haymow, three sets of heads and shoulders popped up and down from the lions' den, like a weird Whac-A-Mole game in which the moles were armed with piles of snowballs.

Mary Jane popped up. "Got you, Sebastian Nicholas Hinglehobb." Down she went.

Jag popped up and slung a snowball. "Eat snow, Beamer." And she was gone.

Lauren popped up. "Catch this, Pig Boy. And here's one for you, Other Pig Boy." Vanished.

Pop, throw, duck. Pop, throw, duck.

"What happened?" I yelled at Count Bash the Conqueror of the Galaxy.

"We forgot to leave a guard at the fort while we were inside loading water guns and eating sandwiches. They trapped us with our own trap."

I stretched for a water blaster and squirted off a round. No Whac-A-Moles popped up.

Bash fired his squirt pistol. "Aim at the hole. Aim at the lions' den."

Mary Jane popped up, hit me dead center in the T-shirt with a snowball and ducked. "Oof. Hey, that's cold."

I squeezed off another blast of water, this time arcing it into the air and moving the gun to aim the stream. Just before the shot ran out, a blast of spray dropped into the lions' den. Lions shrieked.

Jag, red pigtails dripping, popped up and slung a snowball. Bash pumped off two shots with his water pistol. "Got her," he yelled through a fresh mouthful of snow.

The Whac-A-Moles kept us pinned down. We couldn't get our legs pulled out of hay holes. I squirted off the last water blast. More shrieks. Bull's eye. Or lion's eye.

Lauren flew out of the pit. "I'll grab their guns." She zigged and zagged past Bash's pistol fire, dashed past both of us, yanking up water guns as she went. "Get 'em, girls!" She dove back into the den.

Mary Jane and Jag popped up, each with a backpack half full of snowballs. They pelted us until they ran dry.

Splat. Whap. Splosh.

Bash laughed too hard to say anything, so it was up to Duke Beamer the Hay-Brained to speak for the fort: "We give up! We give up! You win."

We pulled our legs out of the hay holes and stood up, wet, shivering, and shaking. I reached for our coats. Bash shrugged into his. "But I still trapped you, Mary Jane. Look at your gloves. I caught you red-handed."

Mary Jane held up pink-gloved hands palm out. "I knew you were responsible for this."

Bash grinned. "Yep. Red stamping ink from Ma's scrapbooking stuff. I smeared it all over the earmuffs. When you took them from the chicken coop, it stained your gloves. Gotcha."

Mary Jane peeled off her gloves. "Oh no, funny boy, you trapped yourself. When you switched the bread and scarf for eggs, you forgot to leave the blue and green ones in the chicken coop. Only your farm has blue and green eggs. You left both at the Johnsons's after getting ink all over their porch doorknob, which is where I got inked."

"Wasn't me, it was you."

"Let's see your gloves." Mary Jane shifted her gaze to me. "Both of you."

We pulled the gloves from our pockets and unfolded them. Red ink. Bash shook his head. "That doesn't count. I got some on me when I baited the trap with the earmuffs. I had to touch the earmuffs."

Mary Jane stared at me. "And you, Raymond William Boxby?"

"Goldfish," I said. "It was on the Goldfish crackers box."

Mary Jane crossed her arms. "I certainly didn't do it. Why would I pull such childish pranks?"

I raised my hand. "To get back at Bash for the childish pranks he pulls on you?"

They both glared at me.

Whap. Lauren hurled a snow fastball that nearly knocked Bash off the wall.

"You've got a big arm for a girl," he gasped.

Lauren rammed her fists onto her hips and glared. "You've got a big mouth, even for a boy. That's a stupid story."

Bash arched his eyebrows at me. I zipped my coat, shook my head, and shrugged. He wiped snow gunk off his cheek and buried himself inside his coat. "What story?"

"The lions' pit. Traps. Tricks. You're making fun of me, aren't you?" Tears bubbled down Lauren's cherry cheeks. "You think I'm trapped in a pit because my daddy died, don't you? Creep."

Lauren swiped a sleeve across her eyes. Mary Jane moved up and slipped a pink arm around her quivering shoulders.

I squirmed and tried to puzzle any sense out of what she blubbered.

Bash gnawed on another piece of hay. "Nope, I didn't think of that. But listen, Daniel spent a whole dark night in a pit full of hungry lions. God protected him. In the morning, they pulled him out—"

Lauren broke free of Mary Jane, rushed at Bash and smashed her last snowball into his nose. "*Daddy died, and God didn't stop it*. Momma cries, and I can't help. God didn't rescue us. We got packed off here to Ohio. Your story stinks. You stink."

Lauren spun away from Bash, slid down the hay wall and dove through the trap door. Mary Jane ran after her. Jag wagged a finger at us. "I don't know what you boys did, but you're mean." And she was gone too. She forgot to snort.

I blew out the breath I hadn't known I was holding. "What just happened?"

Bash wiped snow from his face with an ink-stained glove. "Dunno."

"Do we go after them?"

Bash shrugged. "Dunno."

"I don't think we get to cross off the fruit of kindness."

Bash tucked up his legs, clunked his forehead onto his knees, and threw his hands over his head, grabbing two fistfuls of flyaway straw hair. I barely heard him moan, "Beams, I dunno."

"So what do we do?"

The Basher let go of his hair and peeked over his knees. "What we shoulda done already."

I thought about that. "Oh. Talk to God. We haven't done much of that this week, have we?"

"With the blizzards, and traps, and Lauren and Tyler, and collecting fruits and everything, I got kinda busy."

"Yeah." I picked at hay chunks from the bale beside me and tossed them past my feet. "You think it will help?"

"Yep. It's His Farmin' and Fishin' Book. They're His stories. 'Sides, He's the only One who understands girls."

"Yeah." I nodded. "Do you think Lauren will come to church tomorrow? Maybe God can fix it then."

"What about us? Do you think we should wait till tomorrow to ask God to fix us?"

I hung my head. "No."

Bash looked past the rafters. "Hi, God, it's me, Bash."

"And me, too, Raymond."

Bash bowed his head. "I made a mess of things. Again. I'm really sorry. I forgot to ask You first."

I bowed my head. "Yes, Lord, Bash blew it again. Help him to . . ." I shook my head. "Dear Jesus, it was me too."

Bash picked up the prayer. "Help us to remember to always talk to You first. So, God, what do we do now?"

In the short time since I'd asked Jesus to live in my heart, I figured out that He doesn't shout. So in the quiet of the hayloft, we shut out thoughts of the bats and birds and mice and whatever else lurked, and told God everything. Then we listened to Him talk inside our hearts. It wasn't all fixed yet. There was going to be a lot to do.

Chapter 23

The Mystery Man of the Chicken Coop

I didn't bother picking up the broom in the chicken coop Sunday morning. The coop looked so clean it was as if the chickens used their built-in feather dusters to clean. Instead, I poked through the nesting boxes to see how many eggs short we'd be today.

I placed a pink egg in the basket. "Maybe if your chickens spent less time sweeping, they'd get more work done."

Bash checked the feed trough and water dish. Full. "Maybe you're not looking in the right boxes."

I placed two browns and a white egg in the basket. "I check every single box. I even looked behind the roost, the straw bales, and the shovel. Could I be doing anything more insane than hunting for Easter eggs in January? Don't answer that."

Bash snickered. "How about riding superboard super-sleds off the chicken coop roof?"

I checked the storage pen in case any eggs fell and rolled inside.

A burlap feed sack moved. I froze. "Uh, Bash?"

"No. Blasting Mary Jane with snow cannonballs with your underwear. Now that was insane."

"Bash?"

"Oh, hey, Beamer, what do you get when you cross a chicken with a cement mixer? A brick layer."

"Bash!"

"What?"

I pointed a shaky finger at the storage pen. "That feed sack. It's quaking."

Bash whirled. The burlap bag quivered. A bundle of pink, purple, and orange paisleys poked from behind the sack.

I lowered the basket to the floor, pulled out a big, pink egg, and raised it, ready to hurl a fastball. "We're not alone."

Bash stomped up to the storage pen. "I can see you, you know."

The pink, purple, and orange paisley thing shifted. The lump disappeared from one side of the burlap bag, but stuck out from the other, nearly toppling it. Bash clamped fists on hips. "Knock it over and Ma'll make you sweep it up."

A blue-gloved hand slid to the top of the back. A second blue-gloved hand followed. The hands clamped onto the bag, stopping it from wiggling. The hands remained on top of the burlap bag. A green wool hat slowly rose between them.

Leaky red earmuffs clamped the hat to a man's head. Two frosty eyes squinted beneath the green hat, the same green hat Bash tossed into the pen four days ago. The eyes darted about as if he expected something else to jump out.

Something did. It bit me.

"Yee-aaaughhh!" I shot nearly through the roof. The egg flew from my hands and crunked against the ceiling.

I looked down. Mrs. Beakbokbok pecked my toes. *Crazy chicken.*

I looked up. Goo with a big, yellow blob in the center, mixed with pink shell shavings, drooled from the ceiling straight for my face. *Splaaoompf.*

The stranger clamped his ears against the echoes of the scream that came from, uh, well, me. A couple dribbles of red ink squeezed from the earmuffs.

The stranger unclamped his ears and hopped from behind the feed sack. He wore Uncle Rollie's pink, purple and orange paisley sleeping bag. "Morning, Bash."

Bash dropped his arms. "Sir Bob, how come you're here?"

"Overslept." He shucked himself out of the sleeping bag, a tall, slouched, wrinkly-faced guy with a white-streaked beard, so bushy he probably could hide a dozen eggs in it. He'd bundled in an assortment of coats and pants and wrapped his neck in a wool scarf silhouetted with deer—Mrs. Pifer's scarf. He tipped an imaginary hat, leaving his real one—Bash's—in place.

Bash unlatched the pen, darted inside, and pumped the guy's hand. "Good to see ya, Sir Bob. You're usually gone by winter."

"Hung around too long. Blizzard caught me." He wrung his hands. "Didn't want to trouble no one."

What a laugh. The mystery man of the chicken coop had caused nothing but trouble all week. I wiped egg yolk from my eyes and nose and flicked the gunk to the floor. Sir Bob flinched. "Just swept that."

Bash burst into annoying cackling. "The yolk's on you, Beamer."

I swiped egg goo from my forehead. "That joke's so old, it smells of rotten eggs."

"Um . . . look who's got egg on his face?"

"Still lame, even for you."

Bash scratched his ear for a couple seconds. "Hey, Humpty—"

"Forget it," I growled. "Who's this?"

Bash grabbed the sleeping bag guy's arm. "Beamer, meet Sir Bob. He shows up summers and falls to help farmers with fieldwork. Sir Bob, the egghead with his brains leaking out is my cousin from Virginia Beach, Ray-Ray Sunbeam Beamer. You can call him Beamer."

"My name's Raymond, and we moved to Ohio four months ago." I held out my mitten, saw egg gunk dripping from it, and thought better about a handshake. "How'd you get the name Sir Bob, sir?"

"Dunno." His clothes billowed and sagged in scraggly bunches. I counted four layers of frayed jackets, both flannel and denim. Thin blue workpants poked through the knee-hole of brown corduroys.

Bash ran over to pull me into the pen. "It's 'cause of his stories. When kids work hay wagons or get stuck in barns, Sir Bob tells stories about being a knight in faraway countries, like England, Spain, Moscow, or Montana."

"Been skipping your geography homework again, haven't

you?" I poked through my pockets, looking for a handkerchief, burger napkin, or old tissue to wipe my face.

"We make up the quest, and Sir Bob invents a story about it, starring himself as a knight for King Artemus of the Round Label."

"King Arthur and the Knights of the Round Table," I corrected.

"Nope. Artemus of the Round Label. Right, Sir Bob?"

"Reckon so." Sir Bob pulled a rag out of an inner coat pocket and offered it to me. Drying egg goo already squeezed my cheeks and eyebrows, so I took it.

"Sir Bob can stretch a story over a whole week of hay baling. You spend a lot of weeks on hay wagons in the summer. It can get boring."

The stranger nodded. "Reckon so." His brambled beard bounced, but nothing fell out.

I tugged at Bash's sleeve. "I need to talk to you. Over there." I waved at the sleeping bag guy. "We'll be right back."

"Weren't going nowhere."

I dragged Bash to the other side of the chicken coop. "Are you *crazy*? I mean, more than usual?"

"What?"

"We caught a thief sleeping in the chicken coop. A thief who's been causing trouble all week. We need to get your dad. Now."

Bash looked around. "What thief? Where?"

"Him. Over there. Sir Whatshisname."

"Sir Bob? He's no thief."

"He's wearing your hat, your earmuffs, Mary Jane's gloves, and Mrs. Pifer's scarf. He's got your dad's sleeping bag. And he's sleeping in a chicken coop. You know what that means?"

"He was cold and tired?"

I waved my arms over my head. "He's the guy who's been stealing the eggs, gloves, and groceries."

Bash turned around and yelled. "Sir Bob, did you steal eggs?"

"Nope."

"See?"

"Took 'em as pay for work, like your pappy'd give me."

Bash put a hand on my shoulder. "Pappy means dad."

I swatted the hand aside. "I know what a pappy is. And I know what a thief is, and he just admitted it. Get your pappy. I mean, dad."

Bash pulled me back to the storage pen, where *Sir Bob* perched on one of the feed sacks. "Tell him, Sir Bob. Tell him you're no thief."

"'Tain't." Sir Bob studied his blue gloves. Mary Jane's blue gloves. "Cleaned the coop. Fed the chickens. Got paid in eggs."

Bash nodded. "Yep. Whenever Sir Bob helps at our farm, Pops gives him money and food. So do the other farmers when he works for them."

"Needed gloves. Needed bread. Paid with my eggs. People need eggs."

Bash paced. "See, Sir Bob doesn't have a home up here. He camps out in the woods. He doesn't like hotels or houses."

I finished wiping goo and handed back the rag. The thief shook it out, folded it, and placed it in one of the many coat pockets. "Don't like to trouble no one."

"Lots of folks try, but he won't come inside. So sometimes they let Sir Bob wait out rainstorms and stuff inside their barns. Some of the moms set out food."

Sir Bob scuffled his feet. "Whittle. Leave carvings to pay for food. Snow's deep now. Only got eggs."

"Yeah, but—"

"See that top coat Sir Bob's got on? Pops gave him that one in October. Sir Bob wouldn't take a new one."

Sir Bob picked straw from the rip in a sleeve. "Don't got to be careful with old ones."

Bash picked up the ugly sleeping bag and shook off the straw. "It's winter, Sir Bob. We can put a cot or a mattress or something in Ma's sewing room."

The bum took the sleeping bag from Bash and folded it. "Rather not. Houses too confining." He set the bag on another feed sack.

Bash popped up. "Hey, all the neighbors are coming over for church in an hour. Wanna come in?"

The bum stared out a coop window toward the house. He shuddered. "Rather not. Too many people." He toed a knapsack from behind the burlap bag. "Still got the Farmin' and Fishin' Book your pappy gave me. I'll read here." He peeked toward the house again. "Wouldn't mind one of your ma's sandwiches."

"I'll bring you one before church starts. And dinner when we come out for evening chores."

The stranger again tipped an imaginary hat. "Much obliged, Bash, Mr. Raymond. Reckon I better sweep that broken egg. Gotta earn my keep." He shuffled toward the broom.

Bash waved good-bye, and we headed to the barn. I held the egg basket, six short this time. "So you're telling your dad there's a thief in the chicken coop, right?"

"It's Sir Bob. Everybody loves Bob. The neighbors worry how he's doing when he's gone for the winter. They wish he'd get e-mail or something."

"You have to tell them when you get the sandwich."

Bash stopped so quickly that I smacked right into his barn-coat back. "I've got a better idea—a surprise party. Sir Bob will get a bunch of sandwiches, and we'll get our whole fruit basket all at once."

"Please stop thinking, Bash."

"We don't have enough time to get a party together before church." Bash chewed his tongue for a moment. "Got it. We'll get everyone over again in a day or two, maybe for prayer meeting, and we'll surprise them with Sir Bob. They'll love it."

Bash counted on his fingers. "That will get, let's see, kindness and goodness for Sir Bob and joy for everyone else when they see him. That's three fruits of the Spirit. Sir Bob's going to love it. Love makes four. What's left?"

He ticked off more fruits. "Sir Bob's really gentle with the chickens and other animals, and that makes things peaceful, so there's two more. And it's going to take patience and self-control to wait for the surprise and not blab, so keep your big mouth shut."

Bash turned back to the barn and grabbed the door handle. "This is superlicious awesome. We'll harvest every fruit of the Spirit with one big party."

I pulled his arm away. "There's a thief living in your chicken coop in the middle of winter. Don't shake your head at me, Basher. Nobody hired him. He swiped a sleeping bag from the garage. He snatched your eggs. He stole Mary Jane's gloves, and food, and other clothes. And he's . . ." I shook my head. "Well, weird."

Bash crossed his arms. "'Don't neglect to show horsepi . . . hosper . . .'"

I sighed. "Hospitality."

"Yeah, 'Don't neglect to show . . . uh, be nice . . . for

by doing this some have welcomed angels as guests without knowing it.'"

I stomped my boot. "He's not an angel. We'd know it."

Bash shook his head. "Nope. If we knew it, then he wouldn't be an Angel Without Knowing It. Duh, Beamer."

"There's a guy in your chicken coop, and you're going to throw a party."

Bash yanked open the barn door and zipped inside. "Yeah, it's going to be fantabulous." He whipped around and held a finger to his lip. "Remember, it's a surprise for Ma and Pops and the neighbors. So don't tell. Promise me."

"I don't know—"

"Promise, Beamer. It's Sir Bob. Everybody loves Bob."

Did they? It looked like I was more of a stranger around here than the bum—Sir Bob—was. "How come I didn't see him last summer?"

"Sir Bob spent most of the summer with the Humphreys, Bennetts, and Johnsons. He didn't work with Pops until fall harvest when you weren't here. Pops missed him. C'mon, Beams, promise you'll let me surprise everybody."

I'd been burned by too many of Bash's great ideas. My stomach lurched as if I stood in a rowboat during a nor'easter. I don't know why I said it. Maybe because Bash blocked the barn doorway. "All right, I promise not to blab today. But you better not get me into trouble over this."

"Thanks, Beamer. It's going to be so cool. You'll see." Bash dashed into the barn. I stumbled inside and slid the door closed. *Oh man, I sure hope I did the right thing. I hope the bum in the chicken coop doesn't steal anything else. Or eat the chickens. My stomach hurts.*

Chapter 24

Homemade Church and Other Disasters

My ears tingle with anticipation when I see some people plunk onto a piano bench. Ears know when they're about to be hugged by pretty music.

Ears do not tingle when Aunt Tillie jams that dinged dining room chair up to her piano. Mine try to pop off like Mr. Potato Head's and run for cover.

Aunt Tillie mashed the keys. "Let's start with the chorus to 'I Shall be Whiter than Snow.'"

It's one of those really old church songs about when Jesus

washes away our sins, our hearts sparkle. Most of the neighbors packed into the living room tried to jump in. We chased the melody up and down and all around Aunt Tillie's piano pounding, and nearly caught it twice before the song ended.

She flipped pages in her songbook, the only one in the house. "How about 'Jesus Paid It All'? Does everyone know that one?"

Aunt Tillie started beating another song to death and we scattered after another tune, trying to settle on a melody while singing about how even though the bad we did stained our hearts red, Jesus scrubbed them clean as snow.

Bash belted out the songs like he knew what he was doing, sometimes landing on the right key, but most of the time not. His singing matched Aunt Tillie's playing.

Uncle Rollie, his bulk sunken into the couch and his eyes closed, sang through a big smile. Mr. and Mrs. Dennison sat beside him, Mr. Dennison wincing at some of Aunt Tillie's and Bash's more creative notes.

Bonkers sat on the floor between his parents. I rubbed my ears like they hurt. Bonk nodded and rolled his eyes, then nearly caught the melody as a snatch of three or four good notes whizzed by.

I figured the kid leaning against the end of the couch must be Bonkers's brother Lenny, who never came around much because he was in high school and didn't play "with babies." He didn't look like he was having any more fun playing with adults, either.

"Here's one. 'Blessed be the Fountain.'" Aunt Tillie lashed at the piano, and we tromped through another old hymn about being washed whiter than snow. Even my dopey cousin must know by now that we had a blizzard church theme going at blizzard church.

The Gobnotters perched on dining room chairs like two worn-out scarecrows. Mrs. Gobnotter tried to sing, but Mr. Gobnotter kept opening and closing his Bible, a Sunday school book and a notebook with lots of scribbling. I figured he wished he was on his tractor rather than about ready to teach a Sunday school lesson in a living room church. On the floor next to their parents, Jig swayed and warbled words not in the song, and Jag sang without snorting.

Aunt Tillie turned more pages. "That was so nice, people. Here's another one—'Sunlight, Sunlight.' We sure could use some of that to melt all this snow."

The Morrises chuckled from Uncle Rollie and Aunt Tillie's easy chairs. Mary Jane sat beside them in a dining room chair, Darla in her lap. They gave "Sunlight" a try, Mary Jane smiling and Darla mixing up the word *sunlight* into *onion lie*.

Some of the other neighbors filled more chairs dragged in from the dining room and kitchen, including Mr. Zimmerman from the next road over, who brought Mrs. Humphrey and her three kids on his tractor with the heated cab.

Lauren glowered next to me. She didn't sing. Nor smile. She didn't even cringe at the sour notes. She just stared at Tyler, parked beside Bash, giggling and crooning a four-year-old's lyrics that made no more sense than baby Darla's words, but made him just as happy.

In a chair beside Lauren, her mother sniffled, sometimes staring at nothing. She didn't seem to hear any of the singing, squeaking, squawking, screeching, or anything else clattering off the living room walls.

Uncle Rollie shifted forward on the couch and scratched his balding head. "I know it doesn't have the word *snow* in it, but why don't you play 'Amazing Grace' for us, Mattie?"

Aunt Tillie launched into a less than graceful but truly amazing rendition that I sometimes recognized. We sang it anyway.

When the last note died a painful death, Uncle Rollie heaved himself out of the couch and fixed the button that popped loose over his belly. "That's pert near the best singing I've ever heard."

Compared to the cows, maybe.

Bash raised his hand. "Now, Pops? Tyler and I are ready."

"Not yet, son." Uncle Rollie paced a slow circle in the middle of the living room. "We couldn't get out to God's house today, so we brought God's house here. We're getting to have church the way the early Christians did in the book of Acts. They met in the homes of the believers and God met with them. That's because the church isn't a building. The church is us."

Bash raised his hand. "Now, Pops?"

"In two shakes of a little lamb's tail, Bash."

Tyler tugged on Bash's sleeve. "You have a tail?"

"No, Little Farmer. I don't even have a lamb. Pops means not yet."

Tyler stopped looking at Bash's backside. "Oh."

Uncle Rollie slow-paced some more. "First, it's time for prayer. What praises and requests do we need to take before the Lord?"

Mr. Dennison raised his hand. "We're all safe and we all have power. And as long as Morris's stock holds out, I can get it to whoever needs it on my snowmobile. Milk and eggs are no problem around here. God hasn't had to send the ravens to bring us breakfast like he did Elijah."

I didn't remember that Bible story. I hoped they didn't feed Elijah worms.

Mary Jane smiled at Lauren. "We met new friends from the South and get to live through their first snow with them. It makes it fun."

Uncle Rollie chuckled. "It's been a humdinger, all right."

My mind raced to the bum in the chicken coop. I raised my hand. "I want to request prayer for . . . someone who's . . . who's having a tough winter." I looked around the room. "I can't say who, but it's a bad problem, and I . . . we need God to fix it."

Uncle Rollie nodded. "God knows the details, and that's what's important."

Lauren glared at me. *What did I do this time? She didn't think I meant her, did she? Oh, man, maybe I should have asked for prayer for her.* I looked Lauren's way again. Grizzly bear eyes nearly tore me open. Eep. *Dear God, how about if I pray silently for Lauren?*

Mr. Gobnotter cleared his throat. "We can praise God that none of us lost any livestock or family."

Lauren stiffened. "Daddy's not here."

Mr. Gobnotter cleared his throat again. "I'm, er, sorry. I meant—"

In slow motion Lauren's mom spread her hand over Lauren's shoulder. "She knows you meant no one was lost during the storm. We almost were. Thank you for helping. It's just been . . ." The words choked off.

Lauren shook her mom's hand away. "God let Daddy be sick for no reason. Now he's gone, Mommy cries all the time, and we had to move all the way up here into a crummy old trailer with holes and a broken furnace. All our snow clothes are yours. All we eat is what you give us."

I figured Lauren had to run out of air soon, the way she

was going, but she snatched half a breath before taking off again. "God didn't wash us whiter than snow. He tried to bury us right out of His sight with snow. And your singing is crummy too."

"Lauren!" Lauren's mom tried to grab her, but she jerked away, smashing into me.

"Ow."

"Watch it, Other Pig Boy." Lauren shot to her feet, ran into the coat closet, and slammed the door.

Lauren's mom slumped and started to cry again. Mary Jane handed Darla to me and disappeared into the closet with Lauren. Aunt Tillie, Mrs. Dennison, and Mrs. Gobnotter clustered around Lauren's mom. The men looked at each other, shrugging and slouching deeper into their chairs.

Mr. Dennison finally slid off the couch to his knees, bowed his head and began to whisper.

Bash raised his hand. "Now, Pops?"

Uncle Rollie waved him off.

Bonkers rolled his eyes. "C'mon, Bash, let's go upstairs to your room so you and Tyler can practice your Sunday school lesson."

Jig jumped up. "I'll help." He ran past the cluster of praying and crying women to follow Bash, Bonk, and Tyler up the stairs.

I studied the men, all of whom seemed to be whispering prayers now. Uncle Rollie looked up at the ceiling, his arms raised. Mr. Gobnotter sat forward in his chair, head bowed, hands folded. Mr. Zimmerman dropped to his knees beside Mr. Dennison.

I searched for someone, anyone, to take Darla so I could get out of there.

The closet door opened. Mary Jane tip-toed over and crouched beside me. "Raymond William Boxby, she wants you."

"Me? I didn't do it. It wasn't me. I wasn't even at school that day." I paused long enough to gulp in a breath. "Besides, I have to watch Darla."

Mary Jane moved Darla to the floor, where the kid giggled and started stacking everyone's Bibles into a tower.

Mary Jane rested her hand on my arm. I flinched. It was the first time she'd touched me with something other than a fast-moving fist. "Lauren wants you to tell her about Jesus."

The psycho girl I met just five days ago wanted *me* to tell her about Jesus, who I just met five months ago? "What about Bash? He's the one who told me."

"She wants you, Ray. It's your turn to shine the light . . . Ray-Ray Sunbeam Beamer."

"Can't anyone around here just call me 'Raymond'?"

Mary Jane scooped my Bible off Darla's tower, jerked me to my feet, and thumped the book into my belly, just about knocking me back to the floor. "Go."

"I'm going. Give a guy a chance to get himself together, will you?" I started toward the closet—mostly because Mary Jane planted both paws in my back and shoved. She didn't have to push so hard.

Now what? *God, you mixed me up with Bash. I don't know how to talk about You. What have You gotten me into?*

I opened the closet door. "Hello?"

Chapter 25

The Psycho Girl of the Coat Closet

I'd never been jammed into a closet with a girl. Actually, I never spent much time hanging out in coat closets. I didn't know which was scarier—a darkened closet crammed with barn-smelly coats, or the angry girl squished against the far wall. She sat, arms circled around her legs, chin dug into her knees, grizzly bear brown eyes growling.

I gulped—but only a little one. "Um, hey, Lauren. Let's leave the door open. Just a little. So we have some light."

Grizzly eyes blinked. "Whatever. Sit."

I dropped onto . . . yuck. Wet boots. Lauren rested on a folded-up parka she'd yanked off a hanger. Mine. "Couldn't you have used one of Bash's coats? That's the only one I've got. I wasn't planning on getting snowed in on this crazy farm."

Lauren tugged the parka from beneath her. "Sorry. Here."

I shook my soggy coat and reached for an empty hanger. The chill of boot slush soaked into my pants. I sighed, folded the parka into a pad, and sat on it.

Packed with coats, boots, hats, scarves, and mittens, the closet smelled like what you'd expect from a wrestling match between a cow and pig. With a nervous chicken as the referee. I swatted a dangling scarf from my face and flicked boot buckles poking my leg. "So, Lauren, nice place you have here."

"Shut up." She shrugged. "Why'd you do it?"

Was I supposed to shut up, or answer? "Um, do what?"

"Give me your sweatshirt." She tugged on the sweatshirt she wore. "This. The day you attacked us with the big red pig."

"Oh, the rescue mission." I poked my glasses up my nose. "I don't know. You were cold. I didn't need both a sweatshirt and a coat."

"It was your Christmas present." Lauren stared at her knees. "It was nice."

She relaxed a bit until our shoes touched in the semi-darkness of the closet. We both jerked our knees to our chests. I scooted backward, slid off the folded parka, and splashed into another boot slush puddle. Great.

Lauren dug into the pocket of a coat grazing her face, tugged out a ski mask and tossed it to me. "Sop up that puddle with this. It's the hat Pig Boy gave my mom on Pig Day."

While I mopped around me, Lauren twisted a finger into her black hair. "What I mean is you don't want to be here either. It drives you crazy. But you're not sad. You do nice things, even when I yell at you. Why?"

"You should have seen me when I spent all of last summer on this wacky farm with my weirdo cousin."

"So, what happened?"

I dropped Bash's ski mask to the floor and flicked another boot buckle. *God, how do I say this?*

"Well, I let Jesus into my heart. It's like, I don't know, like I was living in a dark closet like this. He flipped on the light. Mopped up the puddles. No, wait—it was more like He opened the door and led me out into the sunshine to play. And not stupid games, either, but good things, fun stuff, smart stuff, really important, super big—"

"You're babbling, Other Pig Boy."

"I'm nervous. You're not going to thwack my nose, are you?"

"No. Maybe. So God loves you?"

I covered my nose. "Well . . . yes."

Lauren swatted a coat sleeve. "God hates me."

"No, He doesn't. He loves all of us."

Grizzly bear eyes clawed me. "So why'd He kill my daddy? He hates me, He hates my mom, and I bet He even hates Tyler. How can you sit there in barn boot water and dare to say that God loves me?"

"He just does, that's all." *Oh, that was a brilliant answer, Raymond. And ducks quack because they don't know how to bark. What a genius.* "I mean, it's just that, well, you see—"

"Yeah, thought so. You can't, because He doesn't. God made a bunch of bad stuff happen for no reason."

"Lauren, God always has a reason. And sometimes, we just do stupid things."

A vicious leg shot out. Lauren stomped my toe. "So you're saying it's my fault my dad died? I killed my dad? You're a jerk, Ray."

I grabbed at my toe, causing my Bible to slide from my lap. I caught it just before it landed in the splash zone. "Lauren, no, I didn't mean that. What I meant was . . ." *How come she didn't ask Bash? He'd probably tell one of his stories and—*

Lauren slumped against the wall. The colorful sweatshirt rippled.

That's it.

I straightened and whipped open the Bible. "Listen, you know how Bash calls this his Farmin' and Fishin' Book? It's because God wrote so many stories about farmers, and Jesus wanted us to be fishers of men." I thumbed the pages. "I remember one story—it's at the front of the Bible, in Genesis, I think—about a kid named Joseph. It starts in . . ." I flipped more pages. "Yeah, here it is. Chapter 37."

I scooted around so Lauren could see the book, took a deep breath, and prepared to do my best Bash imitation.

"See, Joseph was a sheep farmer. It says here he was seventeen years old and his dad, Jacob, had gobs of sheep. Joseph kept telling his ten big brothers about dreams he had at night that they'd all take orders from him someday. Plus, Jacob made him a robe of many colors—like my sweatshirt that you're wearing. His brothers thought Joseph was the biggest pest in the world."

Lauren shook her head. "Not as pesky as two Pig Boys I know."

"Forget the pigs, Lauren. These are sheep farmers."

Lauren picked up the Bible and squinted at it while I told the story as best as I could remember.

"His brothers hated him. They threw him into an old, dried up well—"

"Pit." Lauren smacked the open Bible. "It says right here, pit."

"Yeah, okay, a pit. A trap. Something. Anyway, when a bunch of traders came through, they pulled Joseph out and sold him. Then the big brothers ripped up that robe of many colors, dunked it in goat's blood—"

"Eew."

"—and told their dad that they found the robe and figured that a wild animal must have eaten Joseph."

Lauren nodded. "So they get rid of the pest and get some cash too. Cool."

"No, it's not cool. They just sold their little brother. Would you sell Tyler at the mall? And tell your mom the snake at the pet store ate him?"

"No, I guess not."

I poked the closet door open a bit more. "Anyway, Joseph ended up in Egypt—"

"Where?"

"Egypt. It's a country."

Lauren pushed the Bible at me. "No, where in here? The next chapter is about somebody named Judah."

She was right. "Judah's one of the brothers." I flipped a page. "Here we go. We get back to Joseph in Chapter 39." I handed her the Bible. "See, it says that the head of the security force for Pharaoh—"

"Who?"

"The king of Egypt."

"So why don't they say king?"

"Because they call him Pharaoh. Look, are you going to listen or not?"

Lauren sunk down and her lower lip jutted out. "Fine. I'll listen, Other Pig Boy."

"Stop calling me that. Anyway, the security captain bought Joseph to work for him. He worked so hard that the captain made him boss of the whole big house. Then the captain's wife tried to get Joseph to do some bad stuff. Joseph wouldn't, so she got mad, lied that he did, and had her husband throw him in prison."

"Not a very cheery story, Other Pig Boy."

"Stop . . . Oh, just listen. Even in prison, hundreds of miles from home because of jerk-face brothers, and probably wondering sometimes if God hated him, Joseph did his best. Pretty soon—"

Lauren jammed her finger on the page. "Here it is, verse 22: The warden put all the prisoners who were in the prison under Joseph's authority, and he was responsible for everything that was done there. The warden did not bother with anything under Joseph's authority, because the Lord was with him, and the Lord made everything that he did successful." She looked up. "So?"

"So God had a plan all along. Look at what comes next. Pharaoh had a bunch of weird dreams and nobody could tell him what they meant. But Joseph could because God told him: Egypt's farms would have great crops for seven years, then rotten crops the seven years after that.

"Pharaoh made Joseph the vice president king and told him to build big barns to save all the extra grain from the good years. The plan worked, and all the other countries had to go to Egypt to buy food in the bad years."

Lauren flipped pages. "I think I know where this is going.

Yep, here it is. The bad big brothers had to buy grain from Joseph."

I nodded. "It was like twenty years later. His brothers didn't recognize Joseph grown up and dressed like a vice president king. They bowed, just like in the pesky dream he had about them."

Lauren grinned. "That's when Joseph got them good, huh?"

"That's what they thought when Joseph finally told them who he was. They were shaking in their sandals. But he hugged the jerks and told them to go get their dad and move all their families to Egypt. So not one of them starved to death."

Lauren shook her head. "He should have zapped them."

I took the Bible and looked for the verse I remembered. When I found it, I handed the Bible back to her. "Here, way up in chapter 50. Read what he tells them in verse 20."

Lauren's black hair bounced across the page as she hunched over the Bible. "You planned evil against me; God planned it for good to bring about the present result—the survival of many people."

"See, God used bad things to save a lot of lives."

She looked up. "So my dad died because . . . ?"

I shrugged. "I don't know. It stinks. But God knows what He's doing."

"That's a dumb story."

I pushed the buckle boot aside and sat up. "Wait, there was a verse I had to learn for Sunday school last month. What was it again? Oh, yeah, Romans 8:28: We know that all things work together for the good of those who love God: those who are called according to His purpose."

Wow. Memory verses come in handy after all.

I tapped on the toe of Lauren's shoe to get her to move her foot out of my way. "Maybe you'll just have to ask God why when you get to heaven." A bad thought struck me. "Lauren, you are going to heaven aren't you?"

She closed my Bible and handed it back. "I don't know. I don't know if I want to."

I looked for a dry place. Snow juice everywhere. So I balanced God's Word on my knees. "Yeah, I didn't know if I wanted to go to heaven, either."

"What happened?"

"Bash. I wondered why he was so happy all the time."

Lauren rolled her eyes. "Because he's a dork?"

"Well, yes. But he also let Jesus into his heart."

"Say what?"

I flipped open my Bible. "I think I put a bookmark in here somewhere . . . Here it is. Um, 1 John 1:9: If we confess our sins, He is faithful and righteous to forgive us our sins and to cleanse us from all unrighteousness. See, you tell Him all the bad things you've done, and let Him live inside your heart—"

"You're a dork too. You can't unzip yourself and stuff another whole person inside your heart. Didn't they teach you biology at your school?"

"Not that. Jesus, like, fills up your heart or whatever you call that place inside where you know your dad loved you. And He turns on the light so that no matter what weird stuff is going on, you know God's got it and it's going to turn out just right in the end."

Lauren wrapped her arms over her head, scrunching bunches of hair like a crazy hat. "It sounds like mumbo-jumbo. But I don't want to be trapped in the dark."

This was it. "Then leave the closet, Lauren."

Lauren dropped her hands and looked up. Teddy bear eyes. "Okay."

She jumped to her feet, stepped over me, clocking my temple with her knee, and pushed her way out of the coat closet.

"Wait, I didn't mean this closet. I meant come out of your heart closet." But she was gone.

I dropped my head onto my knees. "Dear Jesus, I think I blew it. Lauren hurts, and I think I just said all the wrong things. But you can talk to her. Please talk to her. She's . . . she's my friend. I think. Just go talk to her. Please. She needs you."

"Ray-Ray, why are you sitting in a closet talking to yourself?"

Jig stood in the open doorway, all freckles and fiery hair, wearing his Sunday-best baseball cap, the red one with the words "Jesus Saves" printed in yellow.

"Hey, Jig. Haven't you ever heard of a prayer closet before?"

"I thought it was a coat closet. Hey, c'mon, Bash is gonna do his Sunday school lesson now."

I hoped it had nothing to do with traps. I'd fallen into enough of them this week.

Chapter 26

Zacchaeus, Bash, Sir Bob, and More Blunders

Jig ran toward the living room. I rolled to my knees, soaking them on the closet floor, stood, and stumbled after him. Sunday school teacher Basher led the other kids and the adults into the dining room while belting out the Bible story song "Zacchaeus":

"Zacchaeus was a wee little man.

A wee little man was he . . ."

Lauren's mom kind of glowed with a big, goofy grin I'd never seen on her. It was the first time she looked happy. Her eyes looked a bit like Uncle Rollie's Jersey milk cow Daisy's—big and brown with some sad in them, yet untroubled and peaceful. She must have talked to Jesus about all the bad stuff going on.

"He climbed up in a sycamore tree,
For the Lord he wanted to see."

Lauren's mom squeezed her daughter's hand. Bash marched up to Aunt Tillie's big, ol' china cabinet and kept singing:

"And when the Savior passed his way,
He looked up in the tree . . ."

Lauren's mom tapped Mrs. Gobnotter on the shoulder. "Have you seen Tyler?"

Bash saluted as if shielding his eyes from a bright sun and looked way up about seven feet to the top of the china cabinet. He kept singing:

"And said, 'Zacchaeus, you come down!
For I'm going to your house today,
For I'm going to your house today."

A ceramic blue jay flew from the top of the cabinet and smashed to the floor. Tyler peeked over the edge and waved. "Oops."

Lauren's mom shrieked and Aunt Tillie's eyelid started flapping. Uncle Rollie grabbed a dining room chair and dashed to the cabinet. "Tyler, you come down!"

Sunday school teacher Bash beamed. "See, it's the story of Zacchaeus, the little guy who wanted to see Jesus. We didn't have any trees in the house, so I helped Tyler climb up onto the cabinet because I knew you'd want us to do a good Sunday school lesson—"

With Tyler tucked under one arm like a football, Uncle Rollie nailed Bash with a glare from the top of the dining room chair. "Go to your room. We will talk about this very soon."

"What did I do?"

"Now."

"Yes, sir."

I shrugged at Lauren. She stared straight ahead, not smiling, not frowning, not seeing anything. Mary Jane, fists on hips, mouthed at me, "What did you do?" I shrugged at Mary Jane.

The adults fussed over a giggling Tyler, straightened more bird statues atop the cabinet, and swept up the pieces on the floor.

The other kids snickered, chattered about snowmen and sleds, and started pulling on boots.

Bash paused at the stairway and implored, "Coming, Beamer?"

An unsmiling Lauren stared at nothing.

What a mess the day turned out to be.

It wasn't over.

My left coat pocket bulged with broccoli I'd wrapped in a napkin. I carried a couple chunks of roast and two slices of Aunt Tillie's pumpkin bread in the other. "I don't feel right about this, Bash."

"It's perfect, Beamer. Everybody loves—"

"Yeah, yeah, you keep saying it, everybody loves Bob."

Bash whipped open the chicken coop door. "We're here, Sir Bob. We brought dinner."

A pink, purple, and orange paisley mound stirred in the

storage pen. "Thanks, Bash. Much obliged. Raw eggs ain't so good all the time."

The bum reached for the roast and pumpkin bread. "Thank you, Mr. Raymond."

"Ray. Just call me Ray." I offered the clotted mat of broccoli and napkin from my other pocket. "Maybe you can pick off the napkin pieces."

Sir Bob studied the mess. "Maybe later."

Mrs. Beakbokbok moved in to peck at my toes. I offered her the broccoli. She nipped my thumb and flapped away. "What's wrong with green gunk? You lay green eggs."

Bash set half a baked potato and a few bites of mincemeat pie on the burlap bag. "Guess what, Sir Bob. We're gonna throw you a party."

Bob chewed some roast. "No thanks."

"It'll be great. It'll be a surprise party for Pops and Ma and the other neighbors. They'll be excited to see you."

Sir Bob took a bite of potato. "Rather not."

"We don't have to go inside a house. We can build snow tables. Or how 'bout right here in the chicken coop?"

Sir Bob shook his head.

Bash scratched his ear. "We'll have cake and ice cream. Beamer and I know how to bake. Men make good bakers. What kind of cake do you want?"

Sir Bob picked up a piece of broccoli, turned it in his fingers, squinted, and picked at pieces of soggy napkin. "Chocolate's nice."

Bash clapped his hands. "An' you can tell one of your stories."

I groaned. "He barely talks."

"I told you, Beamer, Sir Bob tells great stories." Bash pulled two napkins from his hip pocket and passed them to Sir Bob. "Tell us one now about King Artemus and the Round Label."

Sir Bob chewed. "'Bout what?"

"Let's see, make it a chicken, and a . . ." Bash whapped my arm. "Name an animal, Beamer."

"Guinea pig?"

Bash nodded. "Yeah, a chicken and a guinea pig."

Sir Bob set aside the pie, covering it with a napkin. He picked up a piece of straw and chewed it while he ran a blue-gloved hand through his bushy beard. A broccoli bit fell out.

"It was on a Thursday, the first Thursday of the month of Bumbleary—"

"Wait," I said. "There's no such thing as Bumbleary."

Bash whapped my arm again. "In the country of Round Label there is. C'mon, Beams, don't you have any 'magination?"

I crossed my arms and slumped against the pen post. "Imagination should make sense."

"Then it's not 'magination. Or fun."

I rolled my eyes. "Go ahead. Bumbleary."

Sir Bob pulled out the piece of straw, squinted at it, and stuck the other end in his mouth. "It was on a Thursday, and King Artemus told his knights to saddle up. In those days, I rode a ten-foot-tall chicken—"

I popped off the post. "Chickens aren't ten feet tall."

Bash put up a hand. "'Magination, Beamer. Go with it." He bowed to Sir Bob. "Continue."

"'Tain't easy to climb aboard a ten-foot-tall chicken in full armor. I stacked three stepladders a'top each other to swing my leg over Lightning—"

"Who's Lightning?" I asked.

"My steed. So I mounted up on Lightning, and King

Artemus told us that a vile, villainous beast been scampering 'bout the kingdom nippin' on ankles and such. He begged for a knight brave 'nough to capture the critter. It 'twas our old foe, the evil guinea pig Harold."

I choked. "Harold? What kind of a name is Harold for an evil guinea pig? Never mind. I'm going to the barn." I stalked to the door.

Bash ran after me. "You can finish the story at the surprise party, Sir Bob. Beamer will be better behaved then, won't you Ray-Ray Sunbeam Beamer?"

"Stop calling me that—Harold."

At least now I knew things couldn't get any more wacko freaky weird.

Wrong.

Chapter 27

Slip-Sliding Away on Frozen Pond

The next morning I wrapped four strips of bacon, a couple biscuits, and a glob of scrambled eggs into a clump of sports pages I'd pulled from the newspaper recycling bin. If the bacon grease wasn't too bad, Sir Bob could read the basketball scores. I dropped the mess into a backpack beside my chair while Uncle Rollie washed his hands in the bathroom and Aunt Tillie clattered some pans into the sink in the kitchen.

Uncle Rollie returned to the table, wiping beefy hands

on his barn jeans. "The plows have about got all the roads opened up. Pert near time to get back to normal."

Bash shoveled ketchup-covered scrambled eggs into his mouth. "*Mmmf*—can we have everybody over for a surprise party then?"

"What surprise? They can look out their windows and see that. Or just hear the plows rumbling by."

"Oh." Ketchup dribbled from the corner of Bash's mouth. Could he get any more disgusting? "Well, how about a snow going away party. Tomorrow? Beamer and I will bring the surprise."

Uncle Rollie arched a furry eyebrow. Bash wiped his sleeve across his mouth, smearing ketchup and egg parts across his cheek. Good thing he had a dog to clean him up after breakfast.

Aunt Tillie slapped the napkin holder on the table. "Sebastian, how many times have I told you to use a napkin?"

"Dunno, Ma. Seventy times seven?"

The nervous tic took hold of Aunt Tillie's eye. It had been going ever since she saw Tyler grinning down at her from the top of the china cabinet yesterday. "Forgiving you and making you do your own laundry are two entirely different things, young man."

"Sorry, Ma." Bash sanded his face with a fistful of napkins. "And about yesterday too. I didn't mean for Tyler to knock down any of your birds when he climbed up the sycamore tree."

The tic sped up. "It was not a sycamore tree, and you don't climb on furniture, cabinets, refrigerators, dryers, tables, desks, lamps, or chandeliers."

"We don't have a chandelier."

"Sebastian Nicholas—"

Uncle Rollie took her arm. "Mattie, the boy and I had quite a discussion about that in his room."

Bash shifted in his chair and winced. "Yeah."

Uncle Rollie refastened a button that popped open on his blue flannel shirt. "The boy means well, but sometimes behaves like he hasn't got a lick of sense. But he found his senses again, right Bash?"

Bash nodded and bit into the clump of napkins. His eyes popped. He spit the napkin ball onto his plate and chomped into the biscuit he held in the other hand.

Uncle Rollie grinned. "I've heard of distracted driving, but the surgeon general never warned us about distracted eating." He sipped his coffee. "You are using common sense, aren't you?"

"Sure, Pops."

"Any plans in particular for today? Anything you need to tell us? Any surprise we need to know about now?"

Aunt Tillie dropped into her place at the table and passed the biscuit basket around again. I took one for me and started to slip a second one into the backpack. Then I looked at the jar of homemade strawberry jam and kept both biscuits for myself.

I opened my mouth to tell Uncle Rollie about Sir Bob. Bash stomped on my foot. I shut my mouth.

Bash grabbed two biscuits. "Then it wouldn't be a surprise. We were thinking of maybe building a snow fort, since we're not grounded. We can have everyone over to see it. We'll have a surprise inside."

Aunt Tillie fixed us with a stare that chilled the warm off the biscuits. "The only reason you're not grounded, young man, is that I told Lauren and Tyler's mom that you'd teach them how to skate on the pond today. There will be no drilling, sawing, cracking, or otherwise boring through the ice."

Uncle Rollie glopped jam onto a steaming biscuit. "It's been so cold for so long that it would take power tools to smash through that ice."

Bash looked hopeful. Aunt Tillie's nervous eye picked up flapping speed. "Don't even think about it. Mary Jane will be in charge of you kids."

Bash and I groaned. Uncle Rollie waved his biscuit, almost losing the jam. "Mattie, I don't even own a jackhammer. And if I did, Bash knows to be responsible and ask permission." He turned to Bash and me. "Right?"

I slunk a bit. Bash glanced around the table. "If I find a jackhammer, I'll ask."

Uncle Rollie opened his mouth to say something but shook his head. He took another bite of biscuit. "After chores, I'll take the garden tractor and blade back out there to clear the new snow from the ice. It'll be a rough surface, but you'll be fine."

I washed down my biscuit with a glass of fresh milk from the barn. "I don't have skates." Finally, a day to stay inside and catch up on my comic book reading.

Uncle Rollie swished the coffee in his mug. "After church in the living room yesterday, the neighbors promised to send over all the ice skates stashed in their attics and garages. Every one of you kids ought to find something to fit. We've got you covered like a honeycomb blanket of bees."

"Um, thanks." I hoped I wouldn't get stung.

"Oh, and here. Maybe you boys should take another couple biscuits and some of that bacon with you. You never know when someone might need it."

Ouch.

Bash emptied his backpack of old balloons, candles, wrapping paper, a spray can of whipped cream, and crinkled paper hats he found in the back of his closet. "We're storing stuff for the party," he told Sir Bob.

Wrapped in the pink, purple, and orange paisley sleeping bag, the bum sat on a bale of straw and watched. "Yep."

Bash stashed the party goods in empty nesting boxes. "It's a surprise, so we'll keep the stuff out here until it's time." Bash tucked the box of birthday candles into the back of one of the boxes. "We'll have to figure out where to hide the cake where the chickens can't peck it. Once we bake it, that is."

Sir Bob chewed on a piece of straw. "When's th'party?"

"Dunno yet. Real soon. Tomorrow, maybe."

"When?" I demanded an hour later.

Bash pulled the barn door closed, and we headed to the house to collect the ice skates. "When we get everybody over. The grownups too. They'll be so happy to see Sir Bob. What a great surprise."

"I don't like surprises. C'mon, Bash, there's a weird guy who tells stories about ten-foot-tall chickens living in the chicken coop. You can't let that go."

Bash slung the shovel over his shoulder. No wind had blown closed the paths he last dug, nor had any new snow filled them up. "If we tell, it's not a surprise, and it's their fruit because they'll feed Sir Bob. We're the ones trying to collect fruit."

"Listen, banana brain, I don't know about you country kids, but in the city, you don't let bums sleep in sheds, especially not ones who steal eggs and bread."

"Sir Bob did chores, got paid in eggs, and bought bread and gloves. He always buys stuff from the neighbors this way. Except at Morris's store."

"It's not right." I grabbed his shoulder and spun him around to face me. "Look, either you tell your folks today, or tomorrow, I will."

"You're a real Douglas Downer."

"Call me names, Harold Hamster—"

"Harold's a guinea pig."

"I don't care. If you don't tell, I will."

Bash sighed. "Okay, if I can't get the party set today, you can go ruin it first thing tomorrow morning. But he's not a thief. He's my friend. He's the whole neighborhood's friend."

"He's a weirdo."

"Look at me, Unca Beamer." Tyler whizzed past on tiny skates, arms twirling like a windup toy.

Mary Jane swooshed past, hands clasped behind her back. "Excellent, Tyler Lewis Rodriguez. You learn quickly."

In the middle of the pond, Bonkers anchored a crack-the-whip line picking up speed. His hands locked over one wrist of Jag, who held Jig with her other hand, who held the Basher. One more pass and Jig let go. Bash rocketed across the pond. Just before slamming into a snow bank, he slid sideways, screeching to a smart stop in a spray of ice chips.

Gasping and grinning, he cupped his hands in my direction. "Beams, you gotta try this. It's *awesome.*"

I refastened my grip to the pier post at the end of the fishing dock and shook my head. "No, thanks. I'm good."

I wasn't good. My skates kept swishing on the ice. The ice was over a pond. A deep pond. If I fell—and I would—I just knew I'd find the one weak spot and crash right through to the bottom. I hugged the post tighter.

Lauren eased alongside me. She tilted her head as if making calculations. "I think if you want to wrench that pole out of the ice, you ought to grab hold toward the bottom. Better leverage."

"Ha, ha. Very funny." I let go with one hand but hooked a leg around the post.

Lauren floated to a stop in front of me. "Pig Boy's pretty good on skates. What happened to you, Other Pig Boy?"

"Stop calling me that. I grew up in Virginia Beach." I nodded at her skates. "You're pretty good on those things."

"Daddy used to take me ice skating."

"In Florida?"

"We have ice rinks, you know."

"Oh."

Lauren toed off into a slow glide around me. "Mom held Dad's picture last night. Lots of tears leaked out, but she smiled. The first time." She tugged at her mittens. "She held the picture tight, smiled, and cried."

"Wow. I'm sorry."

"For what? She smiled. It was an I-love-you cry."

I unhooked my leg, whooshed my feet real fast, and snatched the pole again. I wondered if I could pull myself up onto the dock. I wondered what an I-love-you cry meant. "So she's still crying, but she's better?"

Lauren glided through a figure eight. Big deal. I scratched out a whole bunch of figure ones.

She braked behind me. "She's different. What happened?"

Hugging the post, I looked over my shoulder. "I think she talked to Jesus. She must have let Him help."

Lauren slid backward against the next post. "He's not giving my dad back, is He?"

"No."

"But I should trust Him, a Spirit thing you say wants to live inside me, a guy I don't even think is real?"

"Yes."

"Why?"

My feet tried to escape in different directions. I jumped and wrapped both arms and both legs around the pole. It was hard to talk with my cheek smashed against the freezing pier post. "Well, look at your mom. She's different. That's real, isn't it?"

Lauren hit me with her grizzly bear eyes, pushed off the post, and shot across the pond without saying anything. Rats, I'd blown it *again*. Could this day get any worse?

Bash's voice squealed above the giggles and guffaws. "Hey, I'll be right back. I'm going to get Gulliver J. McFrederick the Third. We can teach him to ice skate. He'll love it."

A pig on skates? Yep, this day just got worse.

Chapter 28

The Ice Skating Pig of the Pond

Tyler swooped in and circled the pier post holding me up. "Is Unca Bash really going to put a pig on ice skates? Really, really and truly?"

"Not if he's smart."

Tyler squealed into the next swoop and circle. "Oh, goody, he's gonna do it. He's gonna do it. *A pig on skates.*"

Tyler figuring that out almost made him a genius compared to the Basher—except that Tyler thought a pig on skates made sense.

Swoop. Circle. "C'mon the ice, Unca Beams. It's fun." *Swoop. Circle.*

I tried a step. The skate slipped, and I hugged the pier post. "Um, no thanks. I'll watch."

Over a snowdrift, the bouncing ball of a knit cap approached. It rounded the curve and the rest of the ensemble appeared. The hat sat atop Bash. Bash sat atop Gulliver J. McFrederick the Third. The rusty barrel of bacon trotted on short churning legs, kicking up clods of snow with his pointy pig's hooves. The hog squealed—I must be crazy because it sounded like delight—at the circus of kids swishing and whooshing across the frozen pond.

The former wooden ambulance sled thumped along behind Gulliver, flipping and flopping as the pig pranced across the path in the snow Uncle Rollie had cleared to the pond.

Uncle Jake O'Rusty McGillicuddy Jr. trotted beside them, barking at the carousel of kids twirling and whirling across the frozen pond.

Jig glided to the edge of the pond where the pile of skates clustered. "A size three, I think." He fished the four smallest skates from the mound and held them aloft by their laces. "Look, Gulliver, just your size."

I wanted to rush over there and tell them all how weird, rotten, and otherwise lemon-looped their idea sounded. But I couldn't abandon my post.

Jig placed Gulliver's left front foot into a skate. "Hey, we need to stuff the toes of the skates. Guys, throw us some of your scarves, hats, and mittens." He popped off the wool hat he wore overtop his baseball cap with earflaps and packed the wool hat into one skate toe and added a wadded-up handkerchief from his back pocket.

Tyler skated up, dug inside his coat and unwound a scarf. *My* scarf. "Here, Unca Bonk. It makes me sweaty."

Jag wore two pairs of gloves, one over the other. She snorted and donated the outer pair to the cause, plus a clump of tissues from her coat pocket. "A pig on ice. Pear head."

Mary Jane and Lauren added another scarf, more mittens, a couple hair scrunchies and a pair of socks. "One should always carry a pair of extra socks in the winter," Mary Jane pronounced.

Soon Jig and Bash stuffed the four tiny skates so full that there remained only enough room for pig hooves and legs—which was the point. Tying the laces, they snugged four skates—two white and two black—onto Gulliver, who snuffled into the snow in case someone dropped any candy bars or ears of corn.

A swine on skates stood at the edge of the frozen pond.

Skating Instructor Bash glided backward onto the ice and clapped his hands. "C'mon, Gulliver. C'mon, boy."

The hog bounded onto the ice. Four legs went four directions, and Gulliver whumped to his belly, spinning like a Frisbee. *"Rweeeeet, rweeeeet."* He tried to scramble to his feet. Pig feet on blades ran in place and Gulliver whumped again. *"Rweeeeet, rweeeeet."*

Uncle Jake leaped around the twirling pork, his doggy nails giving him traction on the rough ice.

Skating Instructor Bash and his doofus sidekick Bonkers swooped in, one on each side of Gulliver. "C'mon, Bonkers, let's teach Gulliver to ice skate."

"Remember, if he's not having fun, the skates come off, and we take Gulliver back to his hutch," Bonkers said. He flashed a grin in my direction. "If we can teach the pig, maybe the pig can teach Beamer."

I hugged my post. "Very funny. What about if I'm not having fun? Somebody help me onto the pier, get these skates off, and take me to my hutch."

Bash and Bonkers dropped to their knees to help Gulliver stand. They steadied his legs and swished them like big brothers teaching a baby to walk. "Slide like this, Gully." Gulliver grunted.

Lauren swooped in. "Let me help, Pig Boy." She took hold of the hind leg behind Bonkers.

Mary Jane slid behind Bash. "Sebastian Nicholas Hinglehobb, this is one of your daffiest ideas yet. But if you're going to teach Gulliver to skate, he might as well learn the right way." She began steering the other hind leg.

I circled the pier post with some practice step-slides, trying to get the hang of the skating thing. I almost let go once. No one noticed. In the middle of the pond, four kids sliding on their knees cranked piggy legs in rhythm. Jig steered with Gulliver's tail. Jag took the front, skating backward, clapping for the rust-colored sausage on skates to keep coming. Jag snorted. Gulliver grunted.

Little Tyler skated in huge circles around the whole traveling circus. "*Wheeeeet.*" Uncle Jake chased after Tyler.

Bash let go of one pig leg. Gulliver kept the rhythm.

Bonkers let go. Then Mary Jane and Lauren.

Gulliver slid a few feet, tried to run, slipped, and crashed to the ice. They helped him up. Skating Instructor Bash lifted one floppy pig ear and whispered something.

The kids got the legs going. And let go again. Gulliver wobbled and started to pick up a leg to run. Bash grabbed the leg. "Nope. Slide, Gulliver, slide."

Bash let go and Gulliver swooshed one leg. Then the others. Again. And again.

The shaggy red pig *skated*.

Tyler zipped toward me. "He dood it. *He dood it.* C'mon, Unca Beam, you skate too."

Outdone by little kids and a big pig. Great. I let go of the pier. Still standing. So far so good. Okay, push off with the right foot, a bit to the side, just like the hog did it . . . *Ka-boom.* I tasted ice.

"You funny, Unca Beam."

"Yeah, thanks. Next show's at three. Good night."

Skating Instructor Bash screeched to a halt, spraying ice chips into my face. "Beamer, I've got a great idea. Another one. Stay there. I'll be right back."

I wasn't going anywhere. Not until someone helped me up, anyway. I wiped ice chips from my face. Bash tip-toed on shore on skate points, grabbed the sled he'd unharnessed from Gulliver and shot out to the center of the pond. Two minutes later, Bash and the hog both screeched to a halt, spraying double ice chips into my face.

"Beamer, grab the sled. Gulliver will tow you."

I rubbed my shoulder, ribs, and knees. "What happened to the fruit of gentleness? Help me up."

"It'll work. Hold onto the back of the sled and let Gulliver pull you. Then start moving your feet. It'll be just like training wheels. Then you let go—and you're skating."

"You're crazy. Help me up."

Skating Instructor Bash grabbed the back of my coat and dragged me toward the sled. "I taught Gulliver. I can teach you."

Mary Jane and Lauren pulled up. "Raymond William Boxby, it would make so much more sense for you to let Lauren and me help you. We'll take your hands, hold you up between us, and put our arms around you so you won't fall."

Holding hands with two girls? *Their arms around me?* "Bash, you're still crazy. But I'm not holding girls' hands. Help me grab the sled."

I pulled my knees beneath me and crawled on all fours to the sled. Maybe that's the pig's secret. It's harder to fall when you're already down.

I grabbed the two sides of the sled. "Bash, are you sure this will work?"

"Nope. But it might."

Chapter 29

Home Again, Home Again in My Snow Bank

I picked up one foot, then the other, planting the skates onto the ice. I hunched over the sled, my back end wobbling high in the air over shaky legs, my front end pressed onto the wooden slats. I looked in front of me, but my whole view was two pork legs in skates, a hammy backside, and a curly red tail. *Yes, this definitely was pure craziness.*

Mary Jane sighed. "Boys are such snowflakes."

I tried to hold my footing. "Bash, this better work."

"Let's find out. Gulliver, *giddyup*."

Pig feet churned. Gulliver took off at a speed slightly faster than a jet. My chin hit the sled and my knees hit the ice. *"Yeow. Gentle fruit. Gentle."*

Skating Instructor Bash whisked beside me and yanked up my backside by the belt loop. "You can do this, Beamer. Move your feet."

I held a death grip on the sled. My feet moved—about sixteen or seventeen directions at once. "Catch me!"

Jig grabbed a fistful of coat on my right and Bash held the left. Tyler pushed. At least I think it was Tyler. Bonkers took the front, leading Gulliver. *"Yeeee-haw."*

I yelled something too. I can't remember what, but I'm pretty sure it wasn't *Mommmmeeeeeeeeee!* like Bash claimed later.

The undignified pig train ripped across the ice. Gulliver skated at about a million miles an hour. My feet slipped wide apart like they couldn't stand the smell of each other. I felt the sandpaper surface of the pond ice from one ankle all the way to the other. *Ouch, ouch, ouch.*

Bash hooted. "Great trick, Beamer. You're a pro."

"Haul me . . . *ouch* . . . up!"

Bash and Jig yanked and my feet slammed together at the ankles. We swirled around the far side of the pond and rocketed down the straightaway for the other end, which looked about three states away, but coming up fast. *"Stop. Stop. Stop. Stop!"*

Skating Instructor Bash released my coat and peeled off to the left. "Go, Beams. You're skating."

Jig unclenched his grip from my right. "Let go of the sled, Beamer!"

My backside whistled in the wind as I flew, my ankles clenched, my chin plastered to the boards, my mittened hands clamped onto the sled sides. There was no way I was letting go.

With squeals of what sure sounded like delight, the bacon on blades swooshed across the ice, gained speed to about two million miles an hour, then three million. Gulliver whizzed around the curve on two skates, one white, one black.

I zinged right out of my mittens. They stuck to the sled. I cracked free and whipped around in more circles than the wheel on a flipped-over bicycle. Round and round and round and . . .

Breakfast rushed up from my stomach but stuck in my throat. At these speeds, even hurls feared to leap.

Ker-Thunk.

My skates hit the edge of the pond. Or the edge of the earth. I wasn't sure. Whatever happened, my feet no longer touched anything. I'd been launched.

I jetted into space. I'd be waving good-bye to the moon any second.

Ka-Woooompf. Nope, not the moon. A snow bank. I knew this feeling. My quivering feet probably twanged like an arrow sticking out of a target. I couldn't hear if they did since my head had burrowed about three feet into the snow.

All because of an ice-skating pig.

Something grabbed me around the ankles and yanked. This time I hoped it was the bear. Another yank and I popped out of the snow.

Lauren, arms wrapped around my skate tops, giggled. "Pretty fancy skating, Other Pig Boy."

I flipped around and sat in the snow, my back against the bank. I was off the ice and staying off. "Stop calling me—oh, never mind."

Uncle Jake bounded up, slurped snow off my face, sniffed

my nose, woofed, and skittered off across the ice. Gulliver glided another lap around the pond. Jig and Tyler rode the sled, while the other kids raced the hog and the dog.

Lauren plopped down beside me in the snow. "Why do you do it?"

Uh-oh? God, help me not to blow it again. "Do what?"

She rolled a snowball and tossed it onto the ice. "Listen to Pig Boy. You know the things he tells you to do are insane, but you do them anyway."

I leaned my head against the snow bank. "Before you tell me I'm crazy, Lauren, you're the one who sat in the snow on purpose."

"I'm wearing snowmobile pants. You're wearing jeans. Guess that makes me the smart one."

I bounced my head against the snow wall. "So you came over to laugh at me?"

"I told you. I want to know why you do it. Why do you trust him?"

"I don't. My cousin's a lunatic. He's nutty and he's going to get my legs and arms broken someday."

"And that's why, even though you have no clue how to skate, you let him talk you into playing crack-the-whip with a sled powered by a pig on blades?"

I rolled a snowball and tossed it onto the ice. It fell short of Lauren's. "I don't know. I always thought he was the mulberry bush monkey." I shook snow off my mitten. "Maybe it's me."

"It's not." Lauren rolled two more snowballs and built the beginnings of a tiny snowman. "Is that what it's like with God?"

"Huh?"

"You know. Do you have to trust Him even when it sounds stupid? Because you know that while it might sting, He won't really hurt you? And it's an adventure?"

I shook my head. There must be snow lodged in my ears because I think a whole new kind of brain freeze got me. "I don't get it."

She planted a third snowball onto her snowman. "Sure you do. You just don't know it."

"Huh?" King of the talkers, that's me.

Lauren scooped up more snow. "Okay, it's like how you don't know how to have fun on your own."

"I do too."

"Name one fun thing you did on your own."

"I read comic books."

"See. You don't know how to have fun. But Pig Boy does. You don't know what's going to happen, but you know it will be exciting. Dangerous, maybe, but nothing you can't handle."

"I don't know that."

"Sure you do. You trust the peach pit."

"Maybe a little . . ."

"Yeah." She pulled off a mitten and poked eyes and a nose into her tiny snowman. She drew a smile. "I think I'm going to do what you said. I'm going to trust Him."

"Bash?"

"No, silly. I'm not a kumquat. I mean Jesus."

"Huh?"

"I hate being locked in a closet. I hate sitting in the pit. If He can help me get out, maybe I should let Him." She looked at me. "So what do I do?"

I smacked my hand against my ear. Maybe I did have snow on the brain. "Do? Do what?"

"What must I do to be saved?"

That sounded just like the beginning of another Bible memory verse. I closed my eyes and searched for it in my mind. There it was, Acts 16:30: "Believe on the Lord Jesus, and you will be saved."

"That's it? Believe?"

I ran my finger through the snow. "Mostly. That's what Paul told the jailer when he and Silas were chained in prison. It's a cool story."

"You need to show me your Bible again so I can read it. What else?"

I scribbled a couple more lines in the snow—"John 3:16." I sat forward. "Lauren, you've heard of John 3:16, haven't you?"

"I saw a football player who wore that under his eyes. Is it a pass play?"

"A Bible verse. Let me see if I can remember it all."

I squeezed my eyes shut and said a quick prayer inside: *Jesus, I know you're in my heart and that we talk on the inside all day. Please do the outside talking too. I can't get this right, but You always do.*

I opened my eyes, stared across the pond, and recited: "For God loved the world in this way: He gave His One and Only Son, so that everyone who believes in Him will not perish but have eternal life."

Then I remembered another one, the only other verse I'd memorized so far. "Acts 3:19—Therefore repent and turn back, so that your sins may be wiped out, that seasons of refreshing may come from the presence of the Lord."

Lauren started a second snowman. "What's that mean?"

"Repent means to change. You promise to quit doing the bad stuff."

"Then what?"

"Then you ask Him to come into your heart and make you a new person. Like He did for your mom."

Lauren nodded and finished the second tiny snowman with another tiny smile. "Then what do I do?"

"Talk to Him. That's what prayer is. He'll live inside you and tell you."

"He'll take me out of the closet?"

"Sure. He won't let you stay in darkness."

Lauren jumped to her feet so fast that I fell over. She hopped back onto the ice. "Don't stay in the snow too long, Raymond." She whirled around and sped off to the group, grabbing Mary Jane's hand to become the end of the whip.

I sat up and shook my head. It must be brain freeze. *Dear Jesus, I have no clue what just happened. Girls are just weird. I think it was good. Talk to my friend Lauren.*

I watched the kids and the pig and the dog on the frozen pond. I'm sure glad Lauren and I didn't get to the part about baptism. I shivered just thinking about getting dunked beneath the ice. Actually, I shivered sitting in the snow. I pulled myself up and started clunk-walking on skates to the house.

Too bad there wasn't a fire.

Chapter 30

Fire!

Sunlight poured through the bedroom window. Even in my sleep, I squinted against the dancing brightness of the noonday glare and crackle and . . .

Noonday? Crackle?

Even before my eyes flung all the way open, I vaulted from the bed and pressed against the window. Flames shot from the roof of the chicken coop.

"FIRE!"

Bash took a full half second to come awake. *"Wha . . . FIRE! Ma! Pops! Fire!"*

I don't remember pulling on sneakers as we bolted from the room. But they were on. *"Fire! The chicken coop's on fire!"*

We crashed down the stairs and snatched on coats as we smashed open the back door. Uncle Rollie passed us. Aunt Tillie shrilled into a cell phone.

I knew it. Sir Bob set the chicken coop on fire. It had to be him. I should have told.

Flames shot high, the whole length of the chicken coop. Waves of heat crashed over us. Sweat rolled down my face even as I ran through three feet of snow in pajamas and sneakers.

It's our fault. We let him burn down the farm.

Uncle Rollie clamped my shoulder and shoved. "Raymond, hose, shed. Get it to the barn faucet. Bash, fill buckets. Go. We've got to get in there."

I sprinted for the tool shed, flung aside rakes, shovels, and brooms, and ripped the garden hose from the hook on the wall. I dashed to the barn, still throwing the coils over my shoulder. I didn't have enough shoulder. I held onto one end and ran, crossing paths with Uncle Rollie and Bash barreling the other direction, buckets of water sloshing.

Why did Bash have to dig such twisty-windy paths through the snowdrifts? Is Sir Bob still inside?

I tried three times before twisting the hose onto the faucet. "Got it." I cranked the water wide open and took off for the other end of the hose, wherever I left it. Uncle Rollie already had it, charging the fire like a knight with a watery sword against a whole herd of hot, angry dragons. Stab. Parry. Charge again.

The dragons roared, spitting more flames skyward. Uncle Rollie and his garden hose sword fought on.

If things didn't get under control soon, the cow barn would go up next. Then the pig hutches. The tractor barn, garage, tool shed, silos, feed sheds . . . The house. What about their house?

I grabbed two empty buckets and pounded toward the house. I could fill them in the bathtub. Somewhere. I didn't know.

What about the chickens? I didn't hate Mrs. Beakbokbok that much. *Don't let her die, God, don't let her die. Not Sir Bob either. Or any of the chickens. Unless the bum set the fire, then . . . No, God, I didn't mean that.*

Sirens. The volunteer fire department station. Only two miles away. Somebody got there fast.

"Raymond!" Aunt Tillie already had the water pounding from an outdoor spigot at the back of the house. I flung the first bucket beneath the crashing water. It took *forever.* It was half full when Aunt Tillie snatched it away, shoved it into my chest with one hand while swooping the other bucket beneath the stream with the other. "Go."

I ran at the fire and flung the water at it. A hiss. Like a snicker. The fire seemed to bellow: *You can't slay me.*

I heard a great *whoosh,* then a *whump* as the roof of the chicken coop fell in. The burst rocketed flames even higher into the sky. A hundred feet? Two hundred? I backpedaled, stumbled, and sat hard in a snowdrift. I watched. There was no hope for anything left inside now.

No hope. Not for the chickens. Not for Sir Bob. Uncle Rollie sagged, but just for a second. Back to the battle.

A screaming pumper truck pounded into the driveway and rammed through as much of the snowdrift as possible between it and the chicken coop. Firefighters dragged hoses from the truck.

Uncle Rollie shouted at them. "Randy! I'm running the tractor out back to crack open the pond with the plow blade."

A firefighter nodded even as he jammed a handle on the hose that opened up a giant stream of water on the fire.

Another fire truck wailed into the drive. Neighbors on snowmobiles. A pickup truck. More guys in four-wheel drives.

The footprints. Like the ones I saw from the top of the chicken coop a week ago. I barely noticed them while scrambling for buckets and hoses. I'd fallen into fresh prints in the snow. I slammed an empty bucket at the closest one. Scrambled to my feet and ran. To the hay barn. Up the ladder-stairs. Through the trap door. Snapped the pull chain on one of the hayloft lights.

"Where are you?" My voice. Angry. Demanding. "I know you're here."

The crackling of the fire echoed from the top of the hay wall. From the top. Where we built a lion's pit. The jerk could hide up there.

I shot up the side of the hay wall and flung myself over the top. Frosty blue eyes beneath a green wool hat peeked from the edge of the lions' den. I grabbed a hay bale from one of our turrets and slung it at him. "You burned down the chicken coop!"

The baled thunked to a stop well short of the miserable looking bum. "Accident."

I yanked another bale. "I knew it."

The bum sank down to his eyeballs. "Didn't mean to."

I charged, ducking rafters as I stumbled across the hay tops with a bale in hands. "Come up here, you rat, you bum, you, *Harold*!" The echo of crackling loudened. Wait. Not crackling. Cackling?

I reached the edge of the pit, still holding the bale. Sir Bob huddled at the bottom, hugging Mrs. Beakbokbok to his chest. Cheryl Checkers, Lizzie Longhorn, Queen Clucken, Polly Pufflecheeks, and a dozen other birds flapped and clucked and strutted and squabbled around him. Some pecked at a pink, purple, and orange paisley sleeping bag.

Tears streamed down Bob's wrinkly, grime-splotched cheeks. The furry gray beard bobbed. "Couldn't get them all. Stuffed a bunch in sleeping bag. Carried them up here. Couldn't save them all."

"You killed the chickens." I grabbed a hay bale to throw at him but didn't want to hurt the birds he hadn't murdered. "The whole farm'll probably burn."

My fingers tightened around the twine of the hay bale. The bum burned down the chicken coop. Him. All because Bash wanted to collect a fruit basket. Bash's fault. Heat stung my eyes. I didn't tell. The minute we found the thief, I should have told. It was my fault.

No! I swung toward Sir Bob. "I hope you . . ."

A massive hand clamped my shoulder. "Ray."

Uncle Rollie's voice. Quiet. Hard as a football helmet. Scary. "Raymond, set the hay down. Put it down. Good. Now back up."

Uncle Rollie dropped to his knees and stretched out a hand. "Bob! Praise the Lord, you're alive! I thought you were a goner." Uncle Rollie called over his shoulder to a volunteer firefighter standing at the trap door. "It's him! Tell the chief Bob's safe."

Sir Bob handed up Mrs. Beakbokbok. "Couldn't save them all. So sorry, Mr. Rollie."

Uncle Rollie leaned over the lions' den full of chickens. "Great granny's gingham cookies, the hay's sprouting chickens." He set Mrs. Beakbokbok down into the flock, took Sir Bob's hand, and helped him out of the pit. "First you, Bob. Then the chickens."

I gaped at Uncle Rollie. "You knew about Sir Bob?"

"Went out and talked to him myself Sunday night after seeing Bash make up a couple of Bob's favorite sandwiches. Nobody else eats tuna fish and cottage cheese on rye."

I backed up and bumped into Bash. He stared at his snow-caked sneakers. "I saw the footprints. I saw you throw the bucket. I ran to get Pops."

Sir Bob hung his head. The glow through the windows from the fire—less of it now—reflected off his beard. "Button popped off coat. Didn't want to turn on lights. I lit candle."

Uncle Rollie stiffened. "There were candles in the chicken coop?"

Bash coughed. "Mine, Pops. For the surprise."

"You sure lit into one, son—with more to come."

Bash gulped. I rubbed my head.

Sir Bob wrung his hands. "Candle dropped. Couldn't stomp fast enough. Fire . . . everywhere. Sorry, sorry, sorry." He hung his head. "Stuffed chickens in sleeping bag and ran. I couldn't fit all." He shuffled. "They hated sleeping bag."

Uncle Rollie unclenched his fists. "I sure wish you would have come inside with me last night."

Sir Bob tugged at ink-stained earmuffs. "Didn't mean to start fire."

Uncle Rollie stared out the window, where the glow of the dying flames faded. He sighed and threw his arm around Sir Bob. "I know you didn't. I'm just jollier than jelly beans that you're alive. But from now on, no more sleeping in barns. You let one of us put you up."

"Was camping in the Rodriguez trailer. Lady and two kids came. Ran. Left hat, scarf and gloves behind." Sir Bob scuffed a boot on a hay bale. "Needed eggs to buy new ones. Worked for them. Like always."

"Bob, please just knock on the door and let us help."

"Don't want to be no trouble."

"You're not." Uncle Rollie shifted his gaze to me. Then to Bash. "They are."

Bash chewed on his tongue for a moment to kick-start his thinker. "So you knew my surprise, Pops?"

"I didn't want a surprise, son. I want to be able to trust you to do what's right. That shouldn't be a surprise."

Bob shivered. Uncle Rollie unzipped his coat and placed it over Bob's shoulders. Uncle Rollie didn't seem to mind the cold.

"First I made sure that you boys and Bob were safe. Then I waited for you to talk to me. I even asked this morning if you had anything to tell me."

"It's not a surprise if a guy tells," Bash mumbled.

"Bob was a man in need, not a toy. When I couldn't get him to come inside, I took him blankets and a Thermos of coffee. We read the Bible together. I promised to get him to the bus station when the roads cleared. Today."

Bash chewed his tongue. "That's being a hospital . . . I mean, hospitable. Does that mean Sir Bob's an Angel Without Knowing It?"

Sir Bob pulled on his beard. "Reckon I'd know. 'Tain't."

Bash drooped. "Just wondering."

Sir Bob pulled off the earmuffs, studied them, and handed them to Bash. "Want me to pack the chickens back in the bag?"

Uncle Rollie chuckled and led us out of the hayloft. "Bob, I don't think you can get them into a sleeping bag twice. They'll be fine right where they're at for the time being. We'll see about borrowing space in somebody else's coop in the morning."

I arched eyebrows at Bash. He shrugged and tugged at his pajamas collar. I shook my head. I figured he wondered the same thing I did: Would there be space in somebody's chicken coop for us?

Chapter 31

Plucked Fruit

Bash lay on the bedroom floor and tossed a football toward the ceiling. Sprawled across the bed, I fired a ping-pong ball at the spiraling football—and missed.

Bash pump-faked a throw. "Guess you're going home tomorrow."

I bought the fake. My ping-pong bounced off the far wall before Bash flicked the football. "Mom said on the phone that the roads are clear enough to get here. She's probably just afraid we'll burn down something else."

The football floated within a half inch of the ceiling and

dropped into Bash's hands. "Pops took off to the bus station with Sir Bob."

"How come Sir Bob gets off free and we're grounded?"

"It was an accident. But I bet nobody lets Sir Bob sit in their barn anymore."

"At least all the chickens are safe in the Fertigs' coop."

Bash tossed the football. "Yeah. It was pretty awesome to find the rest of the hens in one of the pig hutches. I didn't know Uncle Jake knew how to shepherd chickens."

I flicked another ping-pong ball at the football. Missed.

Bash twirled the football. "So, Beams, how come our fruit farm messed up?"

I tried to juggle three of the ping-pong balls. All three spilled to the floor. "I don't know."

I sat up on the bed, my back against the wall. "Maybe because we did it ourselves."

"Well, duh. How else does it get done?"

I bunched up the pillow and jammed it behind my neck. "Daniel didn't jump into that pit just to prove that God could stop hungry lions. Bad guys threw him."

"Well, maybe . . ."

"He never promised the bad guys that he'd do something that was stupid. He promised God to always do the right thing. He didn't sneak, either."

Bash plucked the football from beneath his head and tossed it. The ball nicked the ceiling. "You're hammerin' me 'cause I made you promise not to tell about Sir Bob, right?"

"Touchdown."

"It's not a surprise party if . . . never mind." Bash tossed the football again. "So how are we supposed to collect all those fruits—goodness, kindness, patience, gentleness, and all that—if we don't make up stuff so it happens?"

I whizzed my pillow at the ball. Missed. "Remember Joseph? He just did the right thing, and God turned it into good stuff."

Bash shook his head. "We didn't harvest any fruit, did we?"

"You get joy. Lauren says I don't know how to have any fun unless you show me."

"Yeah, you're a real bummer."

"Hey!" If I hadn't already thrown my pillow at the football, I would have thrown it at Bash.

The Basher cackled and flung the football. It spiraled within a chicken feather of the ceiling and dropped into his hands. "Other than that, I guess we didn't get a thing right the whole week."

A girl's voice barged in. "You gave up your sweatshirts, gloves, and stuff to a cold mom and her two freezing kids."

We whirled. Lauren leaned against the doorframe. "You sledded the kids to a warm house. You got our car pulled out and our furnace fixed."

She marched in, plucked the football from Bash's hands, and spun it on one finger. "You played with us. You talked to me when I was mean." She giggled. "My brother even calls you clowns his uncles."

Teddy bear eyes caught mine. "And you told us about Jesus."

She flipped the ball behind her back and over her shoulder and caught it. "I guess it's true—boys really are too dumb to know what they're doing."

Bash finally got his mouth to work. "Huh?" That's what I would have said.

Lauren chucked the ball back to Bash. "You banana brains picked your fruit. Just not when you were trying."

Bash fumbled the football. "You were standing in the doorway the whole time?"

"The last five minutes. I always wondered what boys talked about." She picked up my pillow and slung it back to me while still looking at Bash. "I'm on my way to Mary Jane's. Your mom let me come up, but only for ten minutes, since you're grounded again."

She pulled out the desk chair and sat. "I'm really sorry about the fire."

I hugged the pillow then shoved it aside. I didn't want to look like a baby. "It wasn't us." *Oh, that sounded stupid.* "I mean, we didn't start the fire. But, um, it might have happened because of us."

"Yeah, I heard." She spun in the chair. "Anyway, I wanted to say thanks."

"For what?"

"I talked to Jesus last night. I'm not trapped in the closet anymore."

I grabbed the pillow and hugged it hard. "Wow, Lauren, that's *awesome*. So you're okay now?"

"Better." Black hair bounced as she shook her head. "I still don't know why Daddy died. It still hurts a lot. An awful lot. But I'm not alone anymore. I like knowing that God has a plan. Like with Joseph."

All I could say was, "Wow."

"Guess what else? I'm going to learn memory verses too. I found a list in your Bible. I worked on this one last night: A father of the fatherless and a champion of widows is God in His holy dwelling. Psalm 68:5. How's that? Thanks for letting me borrow your Farmin' and Fishin' Book, by the way."

"Wow." Okay, so I'm not great at conversation when I'm stunned. Or overrun by a babbler.

Lauren kicked off into another desk chair spin. "Next I'm going to work on one in Isaiah. It's something about God protecting his flock like a sheep farmer."

"Shepherd." At least I didn't say "wow" again.

Bash flipped the football to Lauren. "So, He's in your heart?"

Lauren spun the ball behind her back and the chair, and zipped it to Bash. "Yep, Pig Boy, He is. Raymond introduced me."

I pushed the pillow aside again. "I did?"

"Yeah. It was nice." She caught me with the teddy bear eyes. "You want me to pray for you guys, now?"

"We don't have to hold hands, do we?"

Lauren shrugged. "Not if you don't want to."

I shoved my hands into my pockets. Bash sat on his. Lauren grinned. "Boys are silly." Then she closed her eyes, and we did too.

"Hi, Jesus, it's me, Lauren. Thank you again for turning on the light. My friends Pig Boy and Raymond are just boys, so they're not real smart. Tell them what they need to know and help them to get it right, because they sure can't do it by themselves. Please let Mrs. Hinglehobb unground them soon so we can play. Thank you, Jesus."

I opened my eyes. "Um, thanks—I think."

"No prob. When you get out, I have a great idea about using shoe boxes to make snow bricks so we can build snow forts. Two teams. Super snowball fight."

She stood. "Pig Boy, I'm going to challenge your snow catapult. I can build a snowball thrower with a baseball bat and fish aquarium net. Can't wait to try it out on you."

Bash whistled. "Cool."

I slid off the bed. "I just wish I knew why God let this mess happen."

Lauren dug her hands into her hips and tilted her head my way. "Remember the memory verse you showed me in Romans? I worked on it last night too: *'We know that all things work together for the good of those who love God: those who are called according to His purpose.'*"

"Sure, but what good's going to come out of this?"

Lauren giggled. "You'll learn not to be such rhubarb pineapple heads. Bye." She dashed from the room and thumped down the stairs.

After a while of staring out the empty doorway, Bash turned and flicked me the football. "I think, Ray-Ray Sunbeam Beamer, we've been told."

I held the football and forgot to remind him to stop calling me that. Finally, I flipped the ball back. "Lauren got saved, Bash. We planted a seed, we watered it, it grew, and now she's a—fruit, I guess. Maybe she's whatever a rhubarb pineapple head might be."

He tried to twirl the football on one finger. It thumped to the floor and bounced under the bed. "Or a fish. God wants us to fish for people for Him. It says so in the Farmin' and Fishin' Book. Girls are people too."

I shook my head. "Nope, she's a fruit. And we're nutcases."

Bash wriggled under the bed after the football. "Hey look, a candy bar. Want half?"

"How long's it been down there?" I wiped my half of the chocolate bar across my shirt and took a bite. A little funky, but not bad. "Bash, I've been thinking."

"Did it hurt?"

"I'm serious. We didn't . . . I didn't do so well with the Spirit thing. I lost my temper. I wanted to bean Sir Bob with a hay bale. I didn't care if it was an accident. I didn't know he'd rescued half the chickens." I picked up the pillow. "Your dad made me apologize to Sir Bob. Guess I needed to. I don't have good self-control."

I winged the pillow at Bash. "And you drive me crazy with that joy thing of yours." I sighed. "Actually, it was kind of fun skating with the pig."

"Told ya."

"Bash, would you, you know, pray with me to get the right Spirit—to be His fruit basket? The good kind."

"Do we have to hold hands?"

"No way."

"Okay, let's pray then."

I bowed my head. "Dear Jesus, please forgive us for the wrong stuff and turn nutcases into fruit so that—"

Bash interrupted. "Oh, and Jesus, let the snow melt on time. We need to baptize Lauren. And we forgot to baptize Ray-Ray last summer when he got saved. We're gonna need to dunk them both all the way under water in the pond in the spring. Gulliver J. McFrederick the Third can help."

A baptism service with a pig and a fruitcake? I hoped for another blizzard.

Acknowledgments

I am blessed from the top of my stocking cap to the bottom of my barn boots with critiques and encouragement from the kids in American Christian Fiction Writers Clubhouse 206—Debbie Archer, Leigh DeLozier, Kate Hinke, Shellie Neumeier, Dawn Overman, Chris Solaas, Cynthia Toney, and Heidi Triebel.

When I lost my mittens and my way, developmental editor Jamie Chavez steered my superboard supersled down the right side of the chicken coop roof. What a great ride!

Mugs of hot chocolate and marshmallows to Tom Bancroft and his marvelously inspired illustrations, B&H Kids editor and summer farm kid Dan Lynch, and the man in the cowboy hat, literary agent Terry W. Burns.

A blizzard of love and appreciation to my wife, Terry Heidrich Cole, whose enthusiastic belief that I could do this snowballed until I believed it too. Look, honey, we have books!

Praise God from whom all blessings flow, including the blessings of laughter and imagination.

Oh, Beamer.

Raymond "Beamer" Boxby is a cranky, city kid who prefers air conditioning and video games to the great outdoors. Unfortunately for him, his parents decide that he will spend his summer vacation with his younger cousin Bash Hinglehobb – at his farm.

Riding cows, sharing a raft with a pig, and chasing skunks are just a few of the things now in Beamer's immediate future. Does Beamer survive the summer?

JOIN THE ADVENTURE TODAY!

In the second book of the Truth Seekers series, Bill Myers combines comedy and suspense to capture the importance of Biblical truths. Project Truth Seekers' crazy invention is a super-holographic replica of Noah's ark.

No problem, except with Noah's ark comes Noah's animals—all of them!

Available in print and digital editions everywhere books are sold.